# TIGER
# IN OUR
# HOUSE

~~ ~~

ANN M PRATLEY

BY ANN M PRATLEY

*Power Moore Investigation Tales*
Hoonigan
Resolution of Happiness
Home by the Sea

*Forbidden Conflicts Series*
Amethyst of Youth
Ruby of Law
Diamond of War
Sapphire of Prejudice
Emerald of Wisdom

*Freedom of Flight Series*
Christian
Brandon
Trinity

*Painful Deliverance Series*
Painful Deliverance
Darkness of Heart
Friendship of Desire

*Golden Desires Series*
The Golden Desires
The Golden Supremacy
The Golden Unity

*Chisholm Manor Series*
Alessandra

# CHAPTER 1

As Alana Templeton rushed around her house in an effort to get on top of what she felt was an endless amount of housework, she experienced a moment of panic. Having earlier established herself as a successful and well-known defense attorney, she'd moved her career aside when she'd found out she was pregnant with her third child. Now that little Tony had reached fifteen months of age, Alana found herself often considering if it might almost be time to return to the workforce.

When she'd given birth to each of her two older children, she'd always returned to her career within a couple of months of them being born. In those years, climbing up the career ladder had seemed like the most important thing she could do. Since the birth of her littlest one, Tony, life seemed different. Before he'd come along, there had been a period when things had seemed more than a little bit uncomfortable in her marriage to Steven. While she hadn't counted on having another child after her first two, she couldn't deny that since she'd announced her third pregnancy, things with Steven had been better. The cloud that had been hanging over them before that news had since disappeared. About that, Alana was glad.

Although the stresses of her work had melted away once she'd embarked on her maternity leave, she often had to admit to herself that being at home could be just as stressful. She had a husband who was supportive and encouraging of her to take as much time as she wanted to focus on being an at-home mom. She was thankful for that, but was it something that she truly enjoyed? Sometimes, she pondered that question for hours at a time, almost to the point of ruminating on it. When she was completely honest with herself, she knew that such questions played on her mind far more than was probably healthy. Each time she acknowledged that to herself, she pushed it from her mind. She had to, just to be able to get on with the next task that, in her mind, simply had to be done.

Moving from room to room, working through her usual rounds of tidying, wiping, gathering, and straightening, she tried to do it all as quickly as she could. As always since Tony had come along, she felt exhausted. She felt like she was on the verge of wanting to lie down and fall into a deep slumber. It made no sense since she'd only woken up a few hours earlier, and her husband and two oldest children had only just left the house. Regardless, it was a way that she often felt during the daylight hours. The only way she knew to keep the feeling at bay was to just keep going.

When she finally felt like the bedrooms and living areas were tidy enough, she allowed herself to take a break. It was a small joy, just to stop doing everything else, make herself a cup of her favorite coffee, and then sit. The sitting was needed from her self-induced speed in running around. The coffee was needed to counteract her body's desire to sleep. That one decent-sized cup of steaming hot beverage seemed such a small thing, but it helped so much with the demands Alana placed on her body, and the constant demands that seemed to plague her mind.

As with every other weekday morning, the break was welcome but never felt long enough. As soon as she'd finished her coffee, she sighed as she returned her favorite cup to the kitchen and then made her move to get on with the laundry. The monotony of the same routine day in, day out, made her ask the same question inside the silence of her head. Was she really happy to be a mother? It was easy to tell herself and others that she did love her kids, but did she love herself when she wasn't working?

Hearing that question in her head, she scoffed. Did it matter if she loved herself or not? She was a mother. She was a wife. Too all around her, she made sure that it was known how much she loved the people in her life. It was her job to do right by them. In her opinion, what she thought of herself was irrelevant. That was what she told herself anyway.

Washing bundled up into the laundry basket, she walked through the living area. The joyful sounds of Tony in his playpen prompted her to smile. She couldn't deny that he made her job easy. When she ran around in the mornings, putting herself under pressure to get everything done and perfect in their home, just as she had done the day before and the day before that, he remained happy in his little space. Both of them seemed to have accepted the morning routine of Alana rushing around while Tony played within the walls that looked like a prison. After all that was done, the afternoons were usually theirs to enjoy together, getting outdoors if the weather permitted, or just staying in if it didn't.

It didn't really matter what they ended up doing. Cold or hot, rainy or fine, the afternoons were the times when Alana focused only on him. It was the only time of day when she truly stepped away from her internal dialogue to focus on someone other than herself.

"You okay, Little Guy?" she asked as she walked past the playpen and opened up the wide glass sliding door. "It's gonna be a sunny one today. How about we move you a little closer to the outdoors while I hang all of this out?"

Seeing the sun beginning to rise, Alana realized just how early in the day it still was. It felt like she'd already worked a half day. The thought of how many more hours she could endure her life in any one day sometimes almost pushed her into a spiral toward depression. To counteract that thought, she forced another smile onto her face. Anyone else might have been able to see how fake it was. The small child inside the playpen wouldn't have any idea.

As she set down the laundry basket on the deck outside the sliding door, she heard Tony laugh. It made her smile harder. She had no idea what he was laughing at most of the time, and she guessed it didn't matter what his little giggles represented. As long as he was happy, she knew she should be too. That was all that she had to keep telling herself as hours and days passed.

The routine of moving the playpen a couple of meters over so that the edge rested directly in the sliding door path was normal for them. Alana wanted to be able to see him, but she wanted him to be safe while she hung the washing on the line outside. Maybe it would have seemed odd to anyone else, but it worked for them.

"You gonna watch me hang all this out?" she asked him as she closed the sliding door right up to the edge of the playpen.

As usual, she heard Tony laugh at her while he watched her walk along the deck to the small ten-step staircase. Getting out in the fresh air was always something that provided a little bit of sunshine in what could seem like long days, even if she only got as far as the washing line.

Taking her time to peg up the laundered items, she made sure to keep glancing at the playpen from where she was. As always, Tony was happily amusing himself. Sometimes he stood against the closest wall of the playpen, casting a watchful eye over her. Sometimes he sat down with his attention seized by one toy or another inside his fortressed little world. Whatever he seemed to do, he appeared happy. In that way, Alana could appreciate that she was lucky. She was well aware there were far more demanding kids out there in the world. Her two oldest had also been pretty easygoing. That, of course, was now beginning to change as her oldest, Bonnie, veered dangerously close to the dreaded age of sixteen.

As Alana thought about what might lay ahead for her and Steven when it came to their daughter having reached the beginning of the stage of independence, she sighed. Sixteen had been the age that Alana and Steven had met. It seemed like more than one lifetime ago, if she was honest with herself. In many ways, it was. Although Alana had plenty of friends who'd already gone through a divorce, somehow she and Steven had held on and loved only one another throughout their many years together. She smiled sadly at that realization. Was that the truth? She wanted it to be. Any wife would. She also knew that she sometimes had to force herself to believe it.

She guessed she should have felt happy at the possibility of having a husband who appeared to love her. She didn't particularly. That was something she told herself was due to simple wariness. She had a husband who had loved her for most of their marriage, but she didn't have the confidence to believe that he had *always* loved her. As usual, on discovering where her mind was taking her, she fought to push the thought aside. Their marriage might not be perfect. That didn't mean she couldn't pretend that it was.

Looking up at the playpen again, she saw Tony once more standing and looking at her.

"To…ny," Alana called out to him while lifting her arm to wave. Inside, she wished she could honestly say that being an at-home mother was as fulfilling as other women seemed to find it. In truth, her real feelings were far from that possibility. Not that she'd ever expressed that to anyone. No, those kind of thoughts she knew she was best to keep to herself.

The smile and laugh that she received from her infant son reminded her yet again to try and feel more positive about life. She took a moment to watch him as he raised one arm and attempted to wave back. It wasn't quite right but in response, Alana delivered him a smile regardless. The best thing about being a parent was watching all the progress that her little ones made, even when they grew up to be not so little.

Lifting the last sheet out of the basket, she

resolved once more to try and focus on the good things she had in her life. They were plentiful and she did know that. Sometimes her emotions just didn't seem to want to acknowledge it. Then there were times when her emotions took her in other directions.

She had down days, just as she suspected everybody did at some point or other. Although she tried to keep them at bay, she knew that there were other days when her emotions took her far deeper than just 'down'. Inside the silence of her mind, she argued with herself, telling herself that it was normal for anyone, but especially for mothers. They worked hard when raising young children in a full-time role. Worked hard and slept little. It was a recipe for sadness, and always had been, for millions of mothers. She was hardly an exception. Yet again, the words were just a form of self-punishment that she put herself through, over and over again, wishing they would stop.

Throwing the last sheet over the line, she took her time pegging one end, then taking the steps necessary to peg the middle and the other end. It was in that moment - right when she placed that last peg - that she heard it. It was a sound that she'd heard before. As she felt her adrenaline begin to rush through her body and her heart begin to pound in her chest, she told herself that she might be imagining it. She'd heard that sound before. Steven would never believe that it could happen a second time. What were the chances? No, it would have to be in her imagination. That's what he'd think. That's what he'd try and convince her was the truth. It was sometimes like that between them - her voicing any of the random thoughts in her head, and him telling her she was imagining whatever had stuck in her mind like an old record on repeat.

When she heard the sound again, she slowly turned. What she knew that Steven would try and persuade her that she was imagining - what she'd momentarily *hoped* she was imagining - she wasn't.

As she remained still, she saw it crouched, resting its full body right down on the ground with its eyes focused on her. For a fleeting moment, her thought went straight to, 'just do it. Just come and do what you want to do to me'. Then she heard the small, happy cooing from the playpen. Slowly, she turned her head toward the sliding doorway. A part of her wanted to tell Tony to be quiet. Of course, she couldn't. Even if she did call out to him in an effort to encourage him to be silent, he wouldn't understand. If anything, he would possibly make *more* noise.

Although, a moment earlier, she'd been thinking that she might be satisfied with her life ending that day, the sound of her son quickly changed her mind. For a fleeting instant, that surprised her, but she knew she couldn't dwell on it. Slowly moving her head again to look back at the predator in her midst, she saw what she wished she hadn't. It was no longer looking at her. Its head had turned and it appeared to have set its sight on something far more alluring.

Alana knew she had to think clearly but quickly. Day to day, among the monotony of housework, her mind wasn't used as much as it was when she was working. That didn't matter. The truth was that thinking was a strength of hers. Thinking and analysis. She was where she was. The predator was where it was. Tony was where he was. Somehow, she had to make sure that at least two of them did not meet.

Despite the attention that Tony was receiving from afar, Alana could see that the animal was taking its time, appearing to be in no hurry to move. Instead of looking like it was eager to kill and feed, it looked more like it was worn out and just relaxing, not unlike a household cat. Not wanting to test how relaxed it actually was, Alana weighed up her options before committing to use all the strength she had inside of her to get to her son. She might not have always cared about what happened to her, but at that moment, she wasn't going to let her son suffer.

She knew there were ten steps from the level she was on, to the level that Tony was on. Ten steps. The number seemed so little. Although she suspected the predator could jump that high without any effort at all, she knew that it was just out of reach as a height that she could easily run and jump up to. In the shape she was in, a direct route wasn't going to work.

Securing her bearings about where the steps were from her, she turned to face the predator once more, setting it in her sights before she slowly moved one foot backward, then another, and then another still. As time appeared to slow down, she maintained her focus on the animal as she continued to slowly take one step backward at a time.

Reaching a point where she suspected the steps must be close behind her legs, she stopped still. The predator's focus was still securely set on Tony. In many ways, that wasn't a good thing. In others, it was. If the predator decided to, Alana knew it could easily jump onto the deck and have her child in the grip of its mouth within seconds. Alana also knew she had to not think about that.

Ten steps. She could run up two at a time, reducing that to five. When she'd taken that five, she'd have to run along the deck to the glass sliding door. She'd have to move the playpen out of the entranceway before she could close the door. She'd have to do *anything* to save her son.

Where were the steps? Her focus was so strongly set on the predator that she knew her mind was scrambling for answers to how to get out of the predicament she was in, along with her son. She didn't want to move her vision, but she knew she had no choice. Turning her head as little as she needed to, she took note of the couple more meters she'd need to cover to be able to get onto the staircase.

Once again, she focused on the predator. It continued to remain still, surprisingly slow to make any kind of move and not appearing at all bothered by anything going on around it. For a moment, it reminded Alana of some of the worst criminals she'd represented in court. She'd often tried to remember why she'd wanted to become a defense attorney. Some of the people she'd worked with had genuinely seemed innocent of the crime they'd been accused of committing. Others had appeared as dangerous as the large being in front of her, always acting cool, calm and collected even though they'd carried out the most horrendous of crimes against other human beings.

She knew she had to keep moving ahead somehow. Refocusing on the direction and distance she'd calculated that the staircase was from her, she inhaled deeply. She might not survive the following few minutes. Neither might her son. Despite knowing the odds were against her, she knew she had to try and at least get Tony into safety. She was his mother. That was the least she should do.

Resolved to give her best, just like she would in any court of law, no matter who she was representing or what they'd done, she turned and sprinted to the staircase. Two steps at a time, she told herself. Maintain focus, and take two steps at a time. One. Two. Three. Four. Five. As she reached the top of the staircase, in her peripheral vision, she saw the predator slowly rise up on its legs. She fought to not stop and look at it. No matter what, she knew she had to move forward. There was no time to consider what the beast in her yard was doing.

As she bounded along the deck, out the corner of her eye she saw it begin to move. Heart pounding, she almost reached the playpen just as she felt the heaviness of the powerful body hit her back, slamming her against the glass. Maintaining the determination to save her son, Alana's adrenaline kicked in to another level. Using the surface of the glass to shove herself and the massive body backward, she gained only seconds to take another step, then lift and fling into the room the playpen, accepting the risk that she might stumble on her son in the process.

Disregarding Tony completely, Alana turned and saw the predator start to leap toward her again. As its head and half of one of its legs passed the line of entry, she slammed the sliding door on it, hammering the aluminum frame against its neck. Face to face with it, for a sliver of time she thought it would easily push the door open again. Instead, it appeared momentarily dazed before then seeming to lose momentum. In the seconds that it appeared to have lost all will to fight for whatever it wanted, Alana seized the moment to use one fist to punch it in the face while she used the other hand to open the door a sliver. She eased it just enough to enable the predator to pull its head and leg back.

As Alana slammed the door shut, she forcefully activated the lock, thankful that Steven had insisted on getting the strongest glass possible for the door. For the moment, the predator seemed agitated but also lacking any real desire to fight, and not at all enthusiastic enough to try and break through. She hoped that if it did try, the strengthened glass would stand up to the claims of the glass door manufacturer. If it didn't, she was a lawyer. She knew how to sue. Then again, if it didn't she might be left alive to follow through on that thought.

Still not taking any time to regard her infant son, she thought about the rest of the house. She gave nothing else a consideration as she ran through the kitchen to close and lock the other outer door, then ran bedroom to bedroom, closing and locking all windows and then securely closing every interior door. If the predator was going to get into the house, she was taking no chances of making it easy for it to move from room to room.

When she finally felt as secure as she could, she ran back to the living room again. On the deck, she could see the predator, growling and looking inwards while slowly pacing back and forth outside the large glass door. It still looked agitated, but it also looked patient, like it had little energy but was still very willing to wait as long as it took for it to get whatever it wanted.

Finally glancing at her son, Alana saw Tony point and laugh at the glass sliding door. Scooping to pick him up, she held him tight against her as tears finally began to flow. The playpen was almost destroyed from her flinging it like she had. Completely out of context to the seriousness of what she'd just been through, her fleeting thought was that she'd created another mess that she, herself, would have to clean up. Inside of her head, she cursed herself again. A mess was hardly of any importance at the present moment.

Outside of their home was something that had the capacity to kill them. If anything about the previous few minutes had gone differently, she and her son might already be dead. As she thought about that, her tears transformed into a deep weeping not of fear, but of relief. She was alive. Her son was alive. Things could have turned out so very differently. Despite how often she had thoughts that she didn't like her life - or at least aspects of it - at that moment, she was glad that things hadn't gone any other way.

After sitting and holding Tony as she forced herself to calm down, she grabbed her phone. Outside the door, the predator remained. Once again, she thought about some of the criminals she'd represented. The looks she'd received from some of them - the look of incredible intimidation - wasn't unlike what she felt she was receiving from outside the glass door. Somehow, over the course of her career, she'd developed a hard skin when dealing with the worst of criminals. It took a lot to make her nervous or afraid - usually.

"Steven," she said, her voice shaky when the call to her husband was answered. She knew there was every chance that he wouldn't believe her. She knew there was every chance that, once again, he'd imply she was crazy to even think it could be true. Even knowing how he might react, she said what she'd called him to say.

"It's back."

# CHAPTER 2

Special Agents Ashley Power and Tim Moore smiled at one another when they met up near the corridor that led to their boss's office. Both had been called in for what they'd been told would be 'an interesting case'. When each had received the call and been told that, although they weren't together, they did both smile in a similar way at the news. Interesting was usually how cases they were assigned were described. Whether it ever turned out that 'interesting' was the right word was debatable.

"Moore," Ashley said when the gap between them closed and they turned to walk down another corridor together.

"Power," Tim replied, quietly teasing her about her usual succinct greeting. He'd have loved to have been able to not speak to her again until she'd started some conversation. In truth, he never could hold out that long. Talking to his work partner was something he did truly enjoy. "How were your days off?"

"Not too bad," said Ashley, smiling at him. "You know me - I always like a bit of peace and quiet between cases if I can get it."

Tim nodded. He'd been working with her long enough to know her quirky demand to be left alone for at least a couple of days after they'd solved a case. It wasn't something that he'd ever seen anyone else need. It also wasn't something he'd ever seen any boss happily provide to one of their workers. For whatever reason, Ashley needed those days between cases, and their boss always seemed happy to grant her the time.

"You'll be rested, primed, and ready to embark on an interesting case then," Tim said, grinning as they approached the office.

"Always," replied Ashley.

"Grab a seat, you two," she heard their supervisor, Sarah Johnson, say when they entered. "You both ready to work?"

"Yep," Tim and Ashley both replied at the same time.

"Good because I have an…" Sarah started to say.

"An interesting case?" Tim and Ashley asked simultaneously, making Ashley chuckle as they both grinned at their boss.

After receiving a look of warning to be serious, both agents said nothing more, instead focusing on Sarah and whatever she was about to tell them.

"Here are the case notes," she said, handing each of them a folder. "You both need to get yourselves sorted pretty quickly. You're booked to fly up there in a couple of hours."

Ashley immediately opened up the folder and glanced over the front page of typed words. When she'd speed-read enough to get the gist of what they were going to be investigating, she flicked quickly through the rest of the pages, expecting there to be something else that might leap out at her.

"This is it?" she asked, surprised. "This is the case?"

Tim looked at his partner, wishing she'd sometimes not speak her mind quite so forthrightly.

"I understand why you look and sound so

surprised," Sarah said, leaning forward over her desk. "But it is what it is."

"We're investigating a *tiger?*" Ashley asked in disbelief. "How ... what ... *why?*"

Tim waited just as eagerly for a reply. They'd completed a few cases that had seemed odd at the time. The notes he'd glanced over indicated something that definitely wouldn't usually demand a standard law enforcement investigation - not by their organization anyway.

"Is there more to this?" he dared to ask his supervisor. "A tiger getting loose doesn't seem like a ... *normal* thing for us to work on."

"I know," said Sarah. "This isn't a normal situation. That's why I've chosen you two to investigate this."

"Because ... *we're* not normal?" Tim asked, feeling unexpectedly bold. His supervisor was many things - fair, solid, and encouraging. She wasn't one to see much as amusing.

Sarah held back the smile that wanted to burst forth. She also held back the desire to roll her eyes at the agent who so often made it difficult for her to keep a straight face.

"I've chosen you two, because you're both good at good at what you do, and I know you'll figure this one out," she said, doing her best to deliver a frown towards Tim. "Now take your notes and go get ready. Like I said, your flight leaves in two hours!"

Dismissed, the two agents stood and walked out.

"Wow, maybe this one *will* be interesting," Tim said as he glanced at Ashley. "I can't say I've ever investigated an ... animal ... before."

Ashley grinned at him.

"I'm sure there's gonna be much more to this

case," she said, knowing the notes they'd received had only detailed the briefest of information.

"Hopefully," said Tim. "But just for the record, I'm more than happy for *you* to conduct the questioning of the accused in this case."

Hearing his cheeky words, Ashley couldn't help but laugh out loud. Whenever they finished a case together, she always needed to be alone and not see anyone, including him. Whenever they reconnected for a new case, she felt like she'd missed his weirdly refreshing outlook and idiotic attempts at humor.

"I'm serious," Tim continued as they pushed open the exterior doors of the building. "You're an exceptional interviewer. I'm happy to be completely hands-off when you go into that … cage."

Ashley smiled at him but didn't reply. In her opinion, he could be an idiot, but he was also a damned good agent, and she knew he always had her back. In general, it took a long time for anyone to gain her trust. Through the number of cases they'd worked on together, Tim Moore had definitely earned it. She couldn't imagine investigating cases with any other partner now that they'd settled into a good working relationship together.

"You picking me up, or you want me to pick you up?" Tim asked her before they would walk their separate ways in the vast carpark. "Assuming you want to go in one car to the airport, that is."

"Yep, one car works for me, and you know the drill, Moore," said Ashley. "I drive - *always!*"

Tim grinned, nodded, and waved at her before walking away. They had their routine. He liked to tease her and pretend that he wanted things to be different sometimes. He didn't. There was much to like about being Ashley Power's partner for investigations. She had a mind like nobody he'd worked with before. That she was incredibly beautiful to look at played no part in how much he appreciated her as his work partner.

"Half an hour!" Ashley called out to him and saw him turn and wave again.

When she climbed into her car, she felt the familiar excitement of adrenalin. It was always the same when she embarked on a new case. Part of her enjoyment in being an agent came from the ability to help people, especially those in need, or those grieving. A greater part of her enjoyment in being an agent came from the thrill of working it all out. Who did whatever was done, and why? She'd never wanted to be a psychiatrist, or a psychologist, or any kind of doctor of the mind, but the human mind did intrigue her. That all humans could be born pretty much the same way, but grow up so different in nature, was an ongoing source of wonder for her.

Grinning, she started her engine and began her short journey home. No matter how many cases she worked on, or how dire the situation she was going to find when she began, she did love her work. Sometimes when she was in her periods of solitude and contemplation, she wondered if she was doing the right thing, making her career such a primary focus of her life. Other people had careers, but they also worked at having a family or even just a relationship around their work. Ashley wanted to only focus on work. The knowledge of that prompted her to ask with increasing frequency if she was going to regret that. Would she wake up years in the future and wish that she'd made more of an effort to meet a nice man and settle down?

Would she wake up years in the future and wish that she'd had some children who could carry on whatever legacy she might leave behind?

They were the same old questions that she asked often. She liked asking questions. It was part of who she was, having such an analytical mind. The frustration that she felt when she asked those particular questions came from the fact that there were never any answers to them.

As she pulled into her driveway, all questions relating to herself were forgotten. She'd briefly skimmed over the details that had been in the file she held in her hand. She and Tim would go over their files more when they were at the airport and then on the plane. It was always their way. For the moment, she acted swiftly in going inside, grabbing her travel case, opening it to make sure there was nothing she'd need that wasn't already in it and ready to go, and then heading to her kitchen. One thing that she'd learned early on in life was the power of good food and good coffee.

Glancing at her wrist, she saw she had just enough time to throw together a very quick vegetable stir-fry, clean up the mess, and then get out the door. After each investigation, she liked to slow down and focus on nothing at all. One reason for that was that she loved to do everything quickly the rest of the time.

As she sat down and scoffed the small bowl of vegetables, she briefly pondered what they were about to embark upon. It involved a tiger and a family. As they'd been told, it could very well turn out to be an interesting case. It was difficult to imagine why a tiger escaping a wildlife park would be something that she and Tim would be sent to investigate, but she knew there was always a reason for everything.

After doing a very quick clean-up of her kitchen, she grabbed her bag and ran out the door. In what felt like no time at all, she was pulling up at Tim's home.

"Hey, hey!" Tim said as he opened the back passenger door and threw in his overnight bag. It was always touch and go when it came to jumping into Ashley's car. She had been known to start moving the car before he actually got into it. Fortunately, that idea didn't appear to be on her mind on that day.

"You ready to go tiger hunting?" Ashley asked him as she began to veer into the flow of traffic.

"I'm not sure about *that*, Ash," Tim said, grinning at her. "But I'm definitely curious about what it is with this situation, that caused Sarah to send us to check it out."

"Agreed," said Ashley. "That is one of the coolest aspects of our job - we never know what could be just around the corner."

Tim smiled and nodded in silent agreement. Whatever issue they were going to find where they were going, it was possibly going to test them to solve it. With a partner who loved analyzing as much as Ashley did, Tim knew they'd get to the end and figure out whatever they were supposed to. They always did.

# CHAPTER 3

After touching down at their flight destination, Ashley and Tim quickly rented a car and made their way to the home they'd been provided an address for. They'd talked about the case notes while they'd been on the plane. As far as they could see, little was actually known about anything other than a tiger had turned up at a family home, scaring them half to death.

"I don't get why there's so little in the file, but we've been sent to come here," said Ashley, her mind eager to get on with the investigating. "Did whoever assembled those notes forget to put in some pages?"

"I agree it is a bit random that there's no more detail, but we're on our way there now," said Tim. "We'll know all about it soon enough. I don't think it's going to be as simple as a tiger just getting loose. It's fair for us to expect there's going to be far more to this story than that, surely!"

Ashley nodded while keeping an eye on the road and checking in with the GPS unit that sat on the dashboard. Within an hour, they were pulling up to the house they'd been instructed to start at.

"Ready?" Ashley asked and saw Tim smile at her and nod.

"Always."

Walking down the path to the house, they each made silent notes about their observations. The house was a moderate home that looked like it had been built around the 1940s, and the path had a slight downward slope to it. Looking around and taking time to listen, Tim and Ashley both noted that while they were in a town, the house they were at was peaceful with more of a rural setting around it. Beyond the house they could see bush rather than other houses.

"Can I help you?" they saw a man ask as the door closest to the street opened.

"Mr. ... Templeton?" Tim asked and saw the man nod.

"That's me," Steven Templeton confirmed. "And you are?"

Ashley watched the body language of the man before them. He looked nervous, as if already aware they were law enforcement and he didn't particularly want anything to do with that. It made Ashley naturally wonder why that would be.

"Mr. Templeton, I'm Special Agent Moore and this is Special Agent Power," Tim explained. "We are here because of a report we received about a ... tiger ... visiting your home?"

As Ashley continued to watch Steven Templeton's body language, she saw him relax on hearing who they were. It was interesting. Moments earlier, she'd been sure that he was someone who was afraid of the law. Within seconds, his body language had changed in a way that made her think that he was definitely afraid, but perhaps of someone or something else, and not of law enforcement at all.

"Oh, yes. Please come in," Steven Templeton said. "My wife is inside. She's the one who ... please come inside."

As Ashley walked into the home, her eyes instantly took in many details about everything she saw. When they'd been shown through to what looked like a large, open living area, they saw a woman holding an infant, and two older children sitting at a dining table nearby.

"Alana, this is…" Steven started to say before he realized he'd already forgotten their names.

"I'm Special Agent Ashley Power, and this is Special Agent Tim Moore," Ashley said, stepping forward to greet the woman.

"They're here about…" Steven began before once again stopping mid-sentence, not wanting to reveal such details in front of his older children.

"Oh," Alana said. "Perhaps we can go out into the sunshine," she added before leading the way through the living area and sliding door, and out onto the deck. "Please sit down. We just bought this outdoor table. It seemed … well, I thought it might be … useful."

As Ashley sat, she studied Alana Templeton. She looked nervous, but she also appeared to be speaking as if she was confused. It made Ashley curious. Despite her curiosity, Ashley's inquiring mind was more than ready to do some questioning to get the investigation rolling.

"I understand you were the one at home when the tiger came here. Can you share with us what you remember about what happened that day?" she asked when everyone was seated. There was so little that she and Tim had been told, that she was hopeful the family would fill in the many gaps that would add up to Ashley and Tim understanding why they were there.

"Oh," Alana said. "Well, I was hanging out

washing ... out there," she started to say as she pointed to where the washing line stood. "And it was ... behind me."

"A ... tiger?" Tim asked for clarification.

"Yes," Alana confirmed. "It just sat there for ages. I knew I needed to get inside to make sure Tony was safe," she added.

As Ashley watched, she saw the woman subconsciously hold the infant even closer to her as if she never wanted to let him go. It could have seemed like an indication of how loving the woman was as a parent, except something about the scene instead made Ashley wary.

"And then?" Tim asked, urging the woman to continue speaking.

"Then..." Alana continued. "Then, after a long moment of terror, I got inside and managed to close the door. After that, I made sure the whole house was secure - as secure as I could make it anyway. I didn't know if it would still be able to get in or not..." she said, her voice drifting off. "Then I called Steven and told him to get the police."

"Why, may I ask, were you sure that the police would be the best people for that situation?" Ashley asked. "Wouldn't someone with animal experience have been better?"

"Oh, yes," Alana replied. "And that did happen ... later. But..."

"It's not the first time this has happened," Steven said, watching his wife grow vague. She'd been doing that a lot since the day the tiger had returned. Increasingly, he worried about her mental state, but he knew he had to make use of the law enforcement that seemed interested in helping them.

"It's not the first time that ... a *tiger* has been

here?" Tim asked, sure he must have been misinterpreting what had just been implied. It was a major detail that didn't appear to have been recorded anywhere in the notes that he and Ashley had been presented with by their boss.

"Yes," Steven said. "Six months ago, it was here as well."

"But where does the tiger come from?" Ashley asked, intrigued. "We thought it came from a wildlife park, but is that right? Or does someone near here own one as a … *pet?*"

"Oh, no," said Steven. "No, three blocks away is the wildlife park - well, they call it that. I guess it's like a miniature zoo, really. They have all sorts of animals, including a couple of big cats."

"And this one has been here before?" Ashley asked for clarification. "To your house?"

"Yes, like I said, it was here six months ago," said Steven.

"And what was done then? Did someone investigate how the tiger got out?" asked Tim.

"No, I don't think so - well, not that we were told about. The first time it got out and came here, I think everyone thought it was just one of those things, you know, where something went wrong at the park and the animal just wandered off," said Steven. "We all thought it was just bad luck that it found our home and tried to get in."

"So that's what happened that first time?" asked Ashley. "It tried to get in then, too?"

"From what Alana said, yes," Steven said as he glanced at his wife.

"Yes," Alana added. "It wasn't as bad the first time. We - Tony and I - were inside. The door was open but I saw the animal before it reached up here.

I was able to easily close it and call Steven for help."

"You weren't at home that day?" Ashley asked the husband.

"No," Steven replied.

"And you weren't at home this time either?" Ashley further asked.

"No," Steven replied again. "I work all kinds of shifts, although usually during weekdays, but I was at the golf course that day. I set aside one full day each month to take part in a small one-day-a-month golf tournament to raise funds for charity."

"And you stay home, Mrs. Templeton?" asked Tim.

"Yes, for the moment anyway," Alana replied. "I was working as a defense attorney, but I've been off work for almost two years now."

Ashley nodded. It was interesting watching the dynamics of the couple. Both seemed to want help, but they equally both seemed extremely vague about what they were offering in the way of information. Just as interesting was watching the body language and interactions as a couple. Were they happy as a married couple, or were they not?

"And, the previous time that this happened, did someone provide any details about *how* it happened?" Ashley asked, all the while continuing to watch each person.

"No. Like I said, someone from the park came and took the tiger back. They apologized and said that it was just an unfortunate event," Steven replied. "We had no reason to think it was anything other than back luck."

"And ... now?" Tim asked.

"Now ... well, you're here," said Steven. "It must

have crossed your mind as much as it crossed mine. What are the odds of this happening twice?"

"Maybe an animal like that … roams to the same place it roamed to before?" Ashley suggested. "If it found its way here the first time quite by accident, is there a chance that it just walked the same route, a second time, out of familiarity?"

She saw Steven look at her as if the idea wasn't brilliant. Regardless of whatever he was thinking in that moment, he did reply.

"To be honest, I don't know," he said. "I wish someone would tell us what is going on. If it's some random back luck, that's not a good thing but at least we'd know for sure."

Ashley nodded while continuing to study the faces of him and his wife.

"Is there anyone that you can think of that would want to hurt either of you?" she dared to ask.

"Not that I can think of," Steven answered, not as if it was an odd question, but as if it was one he'd considered in-depth himself.

"What about you, Mrs. Templeton?" Ashley asked Alana.

"I was a defense attorney, representing a lot of people who did bad things," Alana said. "But I haven't done that for a couple of years."

"No threats have been made against you or your family?" asked Tim.

"No," Alana replied. "I mean, there are always people who are pretty angry about me having provided support to those who've looked guilty of hurting others, but no, I've never received any threat that I considered real."

"And none recently?" Tim asked.

"None at all," said Alana. "I haven't had anything

to do with my workplace, or the courts, or even the police, for this entire time I've been at home."

"Is there anything about this whole situation that you've considered as a possibility about why it's happened?" asked Tim. "It's in the hands of law enforcement, so I'm assuming there's a reason for that."

"I just…" Steven began to say before looking Tim right in the eye. "I just don't know how likely it is that a creature like that gets out twice from the same park, and comes to our house - *our* house - both times."

"Do you have a theory about why it might have happened?" asked Tim.

"No," Steven replied, shaking his head. "I've thought about different possibilities, but none of them really make any sense."

"Very well," Ashley said before standing and holding out a contact card to Steven. "We'll investigate and see if we can find some answers for you. In the meantime, if you think of anything that might help us in our investigation - or if anything further happens - please call."

"Thank you," Alana said as she stood up and passed the infant to her husband. "I'll walk you out."

For a moment, Ashley wondered if Alana was going to share something more with them away from her husband. The expectation amounted to nothing.

"Thank you again," Alana said as she escorted both agents out of the door they'd entered the house through. "I … this idea that it might not be a coincidence is mainly Steven's. If you find anything out - even just to disprove his theory that this has been intentional - please let me know."

"We will," said Ashley. "Thank you, Mrs. Templeton. We'll be in touch again soon."

As the two agents walked up the path, both were quiet in thought. When they'd climbed into the car, Tim turned to face Ashley.

"I'm still not sure there is an actual case here," he said.

"Me neither, but we're here and there's something odd about those people," said Ashley as she started the engine and then looked at her watch. "It's almost five, so probably too late to get into the wildlife park to talk to someone. Check into the hotel, call it a night, and start then questioning the park staff tomorrow?" she asked.

"Yeah, that sounds good to me," said Tim. "Let's go get checked in and then grab a bite to eat. I'm starving."

Ashley grinned at him. Many things changed in their day to day routines and workloads. The one thing that didn't was Tim's appetite.

# CHAPTER 4

"Right, let's think about all of this," Ashley said in her room after they'd bought and eaten a healthy share of takeaways each. "This family get a visit from the same tiger twice."

"Six months apart. Same tiger from the same wildlife park," Tim added.

"Right," said Ashley. "So my first question is, what are the odds of that happening? I mean, even if it got out once, and then it did just follow the same path that it had somehow remembered from six months earlier, how did it get out at all?"

"We should get the answer to that question tomorrow, but at a guess … broken gate latch, maybe?" Tim suggested.

"Yeah, maybe the first time it was something like that, but if you were a park owner and that happened, wouldn't you do anything and everything that you could to fix that gate and make it more secure?" asked Ashley. "It just doesn't add up that it even *could* happen a second time."

"I agree," said Tim. "It does seem weird that this tiger got out even one time, let alone twice. I'm assuming the park staff can't be so bad at their jobs that they don't notice, report, or do something about a problem with an enclosure structure - especially one that houses a large carnivore inside it. I'm also assuming that anyone working with animals like that is going to be highly attentive in everything they do in and around that enclosure."

"Agreed, but … it does seem an extreme way to hurt someone, if it was intentional and it was someone set on hurting this particular family," said Ashley. "Most people who want to hurt or kill someone don't go and use a tiger to do it. A gun or a knife would be easier."

"True," said Tim, nodding. "Then again, we've met some murderers who liked the idea of killing but couldn't stand the thought of doing the dirty work themselves. For some, it's like they want someone dead, but they'd rather someone else did the work for them so they aren't confronted with the sight of the killing."

"I guess sending in a tiger would meet that brief pretty well," said Ashley. "Send a meat-eating animal in, and then the person behind the plan just walks away and leaves the animal to its destruction? I mean, I can see that it *might* work, but it's still such an extreme way to do things."

"Unless the person was someone who knows that tiger…" suggested Tim.

"Or at least knows how to handle animals," added Ashley.

"I guess we'll know more about that when we talk to the park staff tomorrow," said Tim. "For now, the other things we need to think about are who would want to hurt the family, and were they targeting a particular member? The tiger went there when there was one child home…"

"Well, he's a baby, and his mother is at home caring for him all day, every day, from what she said," said Ashley. "If someone was targeting Alana, it could be someone who knows she's at home with only an infant."

"And that's the other thing," said Tim, his mind working through the small amount of details they'd gathered from the family. "Steven Templeton was away from the house on both occasions. He said that he takes one weekday off each month to go and do this charity golf thing, so wasn't there that day…"

"Yeah, but he works full time anyway," said Ashley. "Even if it wasn't that charity golf day, he probably still would've been away from the home, doing his job."

"Maybe. He said he does work shift work, but mostly works weekdays," said Tim as he nodded. "But, yeah, it's not like it was a weekend that it happened on, which it sounds like he doesn't often work."

"The question is, if someone did this on purpose, which parent did they want to hurt?" asked Ashley. "The one who was home or the one who wasn't?"

"Well, either one, I guess," said Tim. "Alana was the one at home. If someone wanted to get back at her for something she's done, killing her or her baby would definitely cause that hurt. On the other hand, killing her and/or the baby could also be a good way to get back at the father if that was the intention of whoever might be behind this."

"And why do it twice?" Ashley asked, her mind busy. When she saw Tim contemplate the question she'd asked, she continued. "I mean, let's say you want to get back at this family for some reason, and somehow you have the means and *weird* desire to do it this way - with a tiger. You try it once, but it doesn't work. Why would you try that method again? You have first-hand proof that it does not work as a method to hurt people. *Would* you try it again?"

"But nobody thought it was intentional the first time around," said Tim. "In all fairness, if someone did this on purpose, they pretty much escaped any suspicion at all after that tiger went to the house that first time. Everybody thought it was just bad luck. Nobody would have been looking for even the remotest possibility that there was someone behind it. Even if, that first time, the tiger had killed the wife and the child, chances are that nobody would have been sought out for committing a murder. At worst, the park might have been liable for some neglect of their animal or something."

"True," agreed Ashley. "But it's so risky to try it again. If you did that, you'd have to expect that someone would question why it happened a second time. The Templetons said that the wildlife park is three blocks away. It's not too far, but when we drove along the main road on the way here, we saw homes between their home and the park."

"Unless tigers *are* known and expected to follow a repeat path," said Tim. "If that's the case, maybe someone was counting on that fact being made known if anyone asked questions."

"Hmm," said Ashley. "I think Sarah was right. This could indeed turn out to be an interesting case."

"Aren't they all?" Tim asked, laughing softly. "Although, to be fair, I've never even heard of anyone in the Bureau investigating any kind of animal - *especially* a big cat!"

"Yeah, it's a weird one, alright," Ashley agreed as her mind speedily pondered all they'd learned so far that day. "Well, I can't think of anything else for us to go over tonight. Tomorrow will hopefully provide us with more answers, once we can talk to the people who know the animal. Meet up for breakfast at 6.30am?"

"Yep!" replied Tim, jumping up and happy to leave her to her space. "See you in the morning. Sleep well!"

# CHAPTER 5

As the two agents sat in the hotel breakfast room with their meals and coffee in front of them the following morning, both were thoughtful.

Before she'd fallen asleep, Ashley had read through the printed file pages again. She'd hoped to glean some more information that she might have overlooked the first couple of times she'd read through it. Her hope was quickly dashed. Everything that was in the file, she had successfully filed away in her memory.

When she'd been satisfied that there was nothing more in written form for her to consider, she'd replayed the entire conversation with the Templetons in her mind. They'd said so little that could be useful, even though their body language had seemed more than a little strained.

"What was your gut feeling about the Templetons yesterday?" she asked Tim as she again mulled the conversation over in her mind to figure out what exactly had felt off about them.

"Not sure yet," said Tim as he stirred sugar into his second cup of coffee. "They seemed … no, I'm really not sure, Ash. They had a traumatic experience - well, the wife did, anyway. You know that sometimes the victims come across as not being the victims at all, just because of their demeanor when we interview them. It's not always an adequate or even accurate way to read what's going on or what's happened."

"True," said Ashley nodding. "But I do think there's something more going on there than we heard."

"Like what?" Tim asked. "What's *your* gut telling you?"

"Not sure, but something's not right," she said and instantly heard Tim laugh out loud.

"Ash, a *tiger* went to a family's home," Tim said, amused at her deduction. "So, yeah, something's definitely not right."

Ashley grinned at him. He could be a cheeky bugger at times, but he was also a great agent. She didn't mind him teasing her at all. Behind his teases was a healthy level of respect that he had for her as his partner. Ashley knew that without any doubt.

"I meant the way that they both sounded nervous, and weirdly as if they were withholding information, smart ass," she said, momentarily reverting to a speaking tone far more often used by children than adults.

"Yeah, I do know what you mean," Tim said. "It's hard to know how anyone would feel after experiencing something like that, though. It must have been pretty traumatic, especially for a mother who had an infant so close by to protect."

"True. Ready to go then?" Ashley asked, purposely timing the question so that Tim hadn't yet finished his second coffee. The look he gave her in response made her chuckle. "Oh, I'll take that stern look as a no."

Tim smiled at her but said nothing. He was just glad to be on a new case with the best partner he'd ever had beside him. He took his time finishing his coffee, just as he always did, before he was ready.

"Okay, let's get out of here," he said.

"Right," Ashley said, standing. "Let's go and figure out what exactly is going on at this so-called wildlife park."

Half an hour later, the two of them climbed out of the car and approached what appeared to be the wildlife park's ticket booth.

"Two adults?" the teenager in the booth asked when Ashley and Tim reached her. "That'll be…"

"That'll be nothing," Tim said as he held up his badge. "We're here to ask some questions about a recent escape of one of your tigers."

"We only have one tiger, Sir," the teenager said.

"Well, then we're here to ask about the escape of your *one* tiger," Tim said, holding back a smile at the boldness of youth. "Is there someone we can talk to? A park manager on duty perhaps?"

"Yes, Sir," the teenager said as she picked up a landline phone inside the booth. "Hi, there are two … umm … cops out here, wanting to speak to a manager." After a brief interaction, the teen hung up the phone and looked at the agents again. "They're on their way here."

"Thank you," Ashley said, briefly worried about Tim making some poor teenager's day not that great with his mock stern approach.

"Hello?" they heard a man's voice call out from beside the booth a few minutes later.

"Hello," Ashley said when she walked around the side of the ticket booth and saw an older man on the other side of the locked gate. "We're Special Agents Power and Moore. We have some questions regarding the recent incident with your tiger."

"Special Agents?" the man asked as he glanced over the IDs held up for him to look at. "Best you come through here then. Easier than you walking through the turnstiles when you don't have a ticket to scan," he went on to say as he unlocked the large padlock and slipped the chain out to enable the gate to be opened. "Not the first time someone's come around and asked about that," he added as he secured the gate again. "It's bad, I know, that any animal could get out of here, but it seems a bit extreme to involve you folk in it, if you don't mind me saying."

"We don't mind you saying that at all," Tim said as they began to walk. "What is your role here, Mr. …?" he asked.

"Oh, sorry. I'm David Simpson," the man said, holding out his hand to shake Tim's. "I own this park. Don't get me wrong, though. I own it, but I don't manage it. I leave that up to the people who really know about animals. I'm just an old guy who likes to think I'm using my life's savings to somehow helping the world and some of the creatures in it."

"But you're here…" Tim said, partially as a question.

"Oh, yes," David replied. "I help out where I can. Most days, I'm pottering around here or there, mostly doing odd jobs around the place. With a background as a builder and general handyman, there's always something that I can do here to help keep it maintained in some way. Animal care, I leave to those that truly know what they're doing."

"So, with regards to the tiger getting out…" Ashley began to say.

"Terrible instance," said David as he turned to face her. "Second time this year, too. Yes, my tiger keeper has some serious explaining to do, but doesn't seem to know anything whenever I've asked him. Maybe you'll get more out of him. I've checked that enclosure over again and again, just in case it's a maintenance thing, but it's sound. I personally can't see how the beast got out, but the staff are adamant it must have just been one of those things."

"Maybe the first time it happened, but surely not two times," Tim suggested and saw the older man nod in what seemed like agreement.

"Like I said, I've talked to everyone who has any kind of interaction with that enclosure," David said. "Nothing's been disclosed to me, but with a flash of those badges of yours, I'm sure you'll get better results."

"Well, we would certainly like to talk to whoever looks after the tiger, if that's possible," said Ashley.

"Yes, of course. I'll take you down to the enclosure now," David said, nodding. "It's about breakfast time for Tigger so you'll get to meet him."

"Tigger?" Tim asked, amused.

"Funny name, I know," said David, smiling. "Kids love it, so it seemed a good idea when he came here as a cub," he continued as he unlocked another gate and secured it again behind them.

"Two gates to get out of the park from the tiger enclosure then?" Ashley asked. "Two gates that are always locked?"

"Yep, should be," David said as he nodded. "Tiger enclosure is just up here," he added as he pointed forward. "And there he is - our Little Tigger."

Ashley and Tim both looked forward, taking in the beauty of the magnificent animal in front of them. It was housed within what they could see was two separated walls of caging. From where they stood, it was difficult to imagine how the tiger could have found a way out by itself.

"I've got an investor appointment in my office soon, so I'll have to leave you here for now," said David. "That's Wayne who's putting Tigger's feed into the cage over there. When he's done and comes out, have a chat to him. I'd be mighty thankful to you if you find out if he's done some kind of wrongdoing. He's a good worker, and investigating him isn't something I'd have initiated or wanted to do, but you're here, so hopefully if there's something I should know, you'll find out what it is."

"Thank you, David," Ashley said as she smiled and then watched him walk away. "Nice enough chap," she said quietly to Tim when they were alone.

"Yeah, he doesn't seem the type to plan someone's murder through the use of a tiger. Then again, I'm not sure who *would* be the type to do something as crazy as that," Tim replied while watching the scene in front of him. "Wow, that is a massive animal, Ash. I don't think I'd be feeling quite right emotionally or mentally after that tried to enter my house either."

"He is beautiful though," Ashley said, redirecting her attention to the tiger keeper spreading food around the enclosure. "That must take some guts, getting in there with an animal like that. But how come the tiger doesn't look at all interested in him being there? What kind of man is our tiger keeper going to be, I wonder."

"Looks like we're about to find out," Tim said as he watched the staff member exit the first layer of caging and then the second. "Hi. Wayne, is it? I'm Special Agent Moore and this is Special Agent

Power. Can we have a word with you please?"

"Yeah, of course," said the keeper. "Wayne Medici," he added, holding out his hand to Tim and then Ashley before seeming to consider how dirty his hand was. "Sorry, probably best I wash up first, and I have to record this feeding in my office, but come with me."

Ashley and Tim fell in step beside the man.

"You're here about Tigger's grand adventure, I assume?" Wayne asked as they entered a small nearby structure.

"We are," said Ashley as she watched him wash and dry off his hands, then pick up a notebook to note something down. "What can you tell us about the instance?"

"Which one?" Wayne asked with a slight indication of a scoff in his tone. "That thing never got out before, and then got out *twice* this year," he continued, shaking his head in what looked like disbelief.

"Do you have any idea how that happened?" Tim asked, watching the man's face. As with all investigations, he found watching people's expressions closely intriguing, and often very telling.

"No," Wayne replied, avoiding eye contact as he indicated for all to take a seat around his desk. "I don't know how, and I don't know why."

"Well, how *would* a tiger get out of that enclosure?" asked Ashley. "It looks like he's in a cage within a cage. Is there some way, that you can think of, that he'd be able to get out by himself?"

"As far as I'm concerned, there's no way that he could do that," said Wayne. "That's the thing that I don't understand. We have two entire enclosures around that beauty. The wire chain netting that you see around the sides and the top also goes underground. It's not just a cage that he's in. He's sitting within a box that's within another box. I've walked around that setup so many times, determined to find any gap that maybe I might've missed. There's nothing. It's like he just walked through the chain netting or something."

"Can you share with us some details about the tiger?" asked Ashley.

"Like what?" Wayne asked, his tone changing slightly to sound almost annoyed at the question.

"Like … he's escaped twice," Ashley said and saw Wayne nod. "He's also gone to the same *house* twice. Why would a tiger do that? Is there something that would make him want to go to a place that he'd gone to before?"

"You mean, did he somehow establish a link to the home the first time he went, and then decide to follow the path back to it because he was familiar with it or something?" asked Wayne.

"Yes, exactly," said Ashley, nodding. "Is that possible … or even likely?"

"Well, he's an animal, so it's not impossible," said Wayne. "How *likely* it is, I can't say. To be honest, I can't tell you how he got out, let alone how he got to where he went - or why. My job is to keep him healthy. That means keeping him *here*."

"But I'm assuming you would have been the one to go and bring him back, since you care for him here?" asked Tim.

"No, actually," Wayne replied. "While I am the person who mainly tends to Tigger, I'm not his caregiver as far as health and wellbeing goes. That's the job of the vet we use - Greg Samson."

"So it wasn't your job to get him back here on either of those times that he got out?" Tim asked.

"Nope," said Wayne, shaking his head. "I didn't even know what had happened till someone told me the following day, when I got to work. I don't know the exact chain of events but, somehow, Greg was the one who was called and he was the one who supervised the transport of Tigger back here."

"Is that normal?" Ashley asked and saw Wayne chuckle.

"Normal?" he asked. "There's no normal about this whole situation. I don't know why or how Tigger got out. I don't know why he decided to go where he went. I don't know what happened that night, once he was away from here. When I came to work to start my shift around lunchtime the next day, he was in the cage and I got on with my job. It was only after someone mentioned that he'd gotten away that I found out. Nobody from above even bothered to call and let me know."

"Hmm," Ashley mumbled as she considered what she wanted to know. "While you're here, are you in or near the enclosure most of the time?"

"Certainly not all the time, but several times a day, I'm preparing to feed him, or feeding him," Wayne said. "At night, he goes into his shelter. That's when the outdoor enclosure gets cleaned out and set up in preparation for the next day."

"Oh, so he isn't in that enclosure overnight?" asked Ashley and saw Wayne shake his head. "Then it wasn't through the chain netting that he would have had to escape from? Is there another door? Another way to get into his shelter?"

"No," said Wayne. "The way it was all constructed means that, for any of us to get into that nighttime shelter, we have to go through the outdoor enclosure. It's a crazy setup, I know, but it is what it is. There's a double slide-door setup on the shelter. That enables us to be safe if we have to get in there to see Tigger at any time in the night - if he's sick or something."

"Right," said Tim. "And when you've been working in the enclosure, have you noticed anyone hanging around and looking suspicious?"

Wayne raised an eyebrow in surprise before answering.

"Not that I've noticed, but to be honest, I'm always keeping an eye on that beautiful creature when I'm in or around there," he said. "This place can get busy, especially on the weekends or when the schools are out. Kids love this place, and especially Tigger, so that enclosure's a bit of a family magnet. When I first started, I used to always be aware of the people who were around. After a while, I just tuned out to them. I hardly notice them now. I've watched Tigger grow up from a small cub so I know he's used to me, but I never lose sight of the fact that he's a wild carnivore at heart. We have a connection and I know how to handle him if a situation calls for it, but I'd never turn my back on him."

"Okay," said Tim. "Is there anything that you can think of that might help us with our investigation into this?"

"No, but then I'm not exactly sure what you're investigating," Wayne said, looking at each of the agents. "To be completely honest, I'm a bit surprised that you guys are even here. Seems a bit of an overkill for an animal escaping from a wildlife park."

"A *tiger* escaping," Tim emphasized. "A tiger that escaped and made its way to the same house twice."

"Is that what this is all about?" Wayne dared to ask. "Is this about our Tigger, or about the people he visited?"

Ashley watched his face for a long while before she decided not to answer the question.

"Well, thank you for your time, Mr. …?" she began to say, asking for confirmation of his name again as a way to distract him from the question he'd asked.

"Medici," Wayne told her again as he stood up. "Wayne Medici."

"Mr. Medici," Ashley said, nodding before beginning to walk out. "Well, thank you. We may have more questions for you in coming days."

"Yeah, no problem," Wayne said. "I'm usually around here somewhere during or after usual park hours."

As they exited the office, Ashley and Tim naturally veered toward the tiger enclosure once again. Standing and peering into the cage, both were thoughtful.

"Do you think there's something off about that guy? Seems a bit blasé about a large animal that was in his care having gotten out," Tim said quietly.

"I agree," said Ashley. "Then again, I've always thought that people in a position like his would love the animals that they care for, as if they were their kids or something. Maybe I've been wrong in that. He certainly didn't seem quite as eager to know what happened as I'd expected."

"Yeah, he was a bit lax, especially considering how he said he'd been Tigger's keeper for so long,"

Tim agreed. "It's quite a beast, isn't it," he continued, peering at the tiger as it strolled in front of them. "I always forget just how big they are."

"He does look beautiful, but I like that there's two layers of security between us and him," Ashley said. "Question still is … how did he get out of there?"

"Well, Medici said that he'd inspected every piece of this fencing and found nothing," said Tim. "I think we can assume that someone let it out. Agreed?"

"Yeah, apart from there being no exit point for the tiger to get out, it's all too coincidental with it being the same monthly charity golf day of Steven Templeton's both times, and the animal going to the same house," Ashley said, looking around. "I'm assuming there must be some security cameras around here somewhere. Let's go and see if we can find out who's in charge of security. Maybe we can inspire them to let us search through some footage."

"Good idea."

# CHAPTER 6

"Mr. Sanchez," Tim said as he and Ashley walked into a small building on the grounds that had been set up for the staff break room and bathroom facilities. "We understand you're the man to talk to about security here at the park."

Ashley watched as the middle-aged man turned, saw them, and instantly looked wary.

"Who are you?" he asked, his tone not at all friendly.

After showing their badges and introducing themselves, Ashley and Tim continued to watch the man.

"We would like to ask you some questions about the tiger escaping from the park," said Tim.

"I don't know nothing about it," Michael Sanchez replied abruptly. "I wasn't working that week."

"Oh?" asked Ashley.

"Nope. I was away on leave all of that week," Michael said. "It wasn't my responsibility. I can't be blamed for whatever happened."

"Okay," said Tim, nodding, although curious about the man sounding so defensive. "Well, we'd love to see any security camera footage of the park from that night - or the whole week if possible."

"I ... I can't do that," Michael said without offering any explanation about why.

"But there *is* footage?" asked Ashley and saw him nod.

"I'm sure there is," Michael replied. "But I haven't got any permission to show it to anyone, and I wasn't the security worker on that week. I'm not interested in getting someone I work with into trouble either."

"Fair enough," said Tim. "Would you rather get into trouble for denying law enforcement access to the security footage?"

It was a daring question, considering he and Ashley didn't have a warrant to be able to demand access to security footage. Even so, it was always worth the time to simply ask. Some people agreed to such things. Others demanded to see a warrant. Tim was glad that, as he and Ashley watched, the man's demeanor changed. After they saw Michael exhale deeply, they heard him sigh.

"Come this way," he finally said, turning to lead the agents out of the space they were in.

As the three of them walked along a path toward another small outlying building, Ashley and Tim looked at one another. They didn't need to use words to convey to each other that they both thought the security guard looked highly uncomfortable. Maybe that was out of fear of doing something wrong. Then again, maybe it was out of fear of what might be seen on the footage. There was only one way to find out.

On entering the building, the agents looked around the small room. Four monitors were on, with each one flicking through three scenes at ten second intervals.

"This is where we can watch everything that the cameras can show us," Michael said as he sat at the desk.

"Watch everything ... and record it?" Tim asked

and saw the security guard nod.

"Yep."

"And these cover all of the park?" asked Ashley as she peered over his shoulder and glanced over each screen.

"Yes and no," said Michael. "They cover each *section* of the park, but not every angle."

"And how long do you keep footage for?" Tim asked.

"We have two hard drives here," Michael answered, pointing under the desk. "The footage is a one-year rolling backup."

"So … that means … every day is recorded over the same day exactly one year later?" Ashley asked and saw him nod again.

"Yep."

"Okay. Can you pull up the footage from the night that the tiger got out?" Ashley requested.

"Yeah," Michael said without enthusiasm. "Hey, I hope I'm not gonna get in trouble for this. I got a family, and bills to pay. I need this job."

"We'll cover you if anything happens," said Tim. "Just show us what you've got."

As they stood back a little and let Michael do his thing, Ashley and Tim looked at one another and then at the screens.

"This is it," Michael finally said. "I assume you mean *this* escape, right? You know that damned animal got out of here twice…"

"Yes, and we will want to look at both nights of footage, but this is good for now," Tim said. "Can you take it back to the start of the night?"

Once the footage began to play, Tim and Ashley watched the order of things.

"That's the keeper - Wayne Medici - encouraging

Tigger into his shelter for the night," Michael said, pointing at the screen as they watched. "Then there is Wayne closing the slide door that keeps Tigger inside, and Wayne walking out of the enclosure."

"And that all looks normal?" Ashley asked.

"Yep, that's what happens pretty much every night for that particular enclosure," said Michael.

"Can you speed the footage up a bit?" Tim requested.

All watched as the video increased in speed and time lapsed more quickly. When the timestamp on the video hit 8:00 am, they observed the slide door opening again in Tigger's shelter. Nothing more happened until they saw Tigger returned to the cage.

"That's it?" Ashley asked and saw Michael nod. "Was anything cut out from that footage?"

"Nope, that's it," Michael said. "Tigger gets put to bed as normal that night. Tigger's slide door opens again at its preset time in the morning. Usually, he would walk out of the shelter and into the closure then, but at that time on that day, he was still wherever he went. Then we see him when he was brought back."

"Okay, so the footage shows when he went to bed, and it shows when he returned, but it doesn't show…"

"It doesn't show him ever leaving," said Michael, nodding. "Just going to bed that night and then being brought back the next day."

"Can you go back to the previous occasion that he got out? Six months ago?" Tim asked and waited for the second set of video to begin playing.

As they watched, they saw a similar routine. Once again, there was nothing out of the ordinary that they could see.

"See. Nothing!" Michael said.

"There must be another way to get Tigger out of that shelter," Tim mumbled.

"Nope," Michael insisted, shaking his head. "After he got out that first time, we inspected the cage section of the enclosure, and then we inspected every board and nail of that shelter. There's no way he could get out from the night shelter at all. *No way!*"

"Okay," said Ashley, stepping back from the monitors. "Can you put the footage for both of those entire weeks onto this for us?" she asked as she handed him a small USB pen drive.

"The entire week?" Michael asked, a tone of annoyance evident in his voice.

"Yes, please," Ashley replied. "Actually, seven days before and seven days after each event would be good."

Both agents remained quiet as they watched the security guard do as they'd requested, all the while sighing as if he'd been asked to do something highly inconvenient. When he handed the USB drive back to Ashley, he stood and faced her.

"I'm not getting in trouble for doing this," he said, his tone verging on hostile.

"No, you're not," Tim said, not liking the sound of the security guard's words. They'd sounded far too much like a threat rather than a simple sentence. "Thanks for this. If we need to ask you anything else, we'll be in touch."

Walking through the park, neither agent said anything more, taking in the sounds and sights of the animals in their enclosures and the substantial flora surrounding the paths right through to the exit.

Once in the car again, Ashley turned to face Tim.

"This is going to turn out to be another case that keeps us guessing, isn't it," she said, making him chuckle.

"They all keep us guessing, Ash," Tim said as he put on his seatbelt. "And yet, we always figure them out!"

"So far," Ashley mumbled as she started the engine. "Okay, well, let's head back to the hotel and have a good look through the rest of this footage. Maybe when we look closer, we'll notice something that nobody else has."

"Yeah, we can do that," said Tim. "When we're back, I'll send all of these files off to the computer forensic team as well."

"You think someone might have doctored them?" asked Ashley.

"Well, that tiger got out somehow, but it wasn't on the recordings we watched, and the guys we've spoken to at the park have said there's no other exit to that enclosure," Tim replied. "I think it's very possible - highly probable, even - that someone's somehow played with the timeline of those clips."

"True. If nothing comes of it, we could be left with more questions than answers," said Ashley.

"Just what you love most, Special Agent Power," Tim said, teasing her.

# CHAPTER 7

After grabbing a quick meal and making their way back to the hotel, both agents settled into Ashley's room with their laptops at hand.

"Security footage files have been sent," said Tim as he put his computer down and went and sat next to Ashley at the small dining table in the room. "How are you going?"

"Everything's set up and ready to watch through, once you hand me that USB drive," replied Ashley, holding out her hand in expectation. "Ready for a lengthy watch?"

"Got the popcorn ready?" Tim asked as he grinned at her.

"You can't possibly *still* be hungry!" Ashley said before she realized he'd been teasing her. "Eyes here!" she added, pointing at the screen and dismissing his mild attempt at humor.

Going through each 24-hour period of the week before the first tiger escape, nothing seemed different on any night.

"I'm guessing that animal care works best with absolute routine," Ashley said, watching Tigger be encouraged into his shelter by Wayne Medici yet again. "Nothing's changing much from night to night, is it."

"No, we're seeing pretty much the same thing happening at the same time, each and every night. But that could mean that we need to be focusing more on the daytime hours," said Tim. "Nothing stands out in this fortnight around the first escape. Let's look through the fortnight of the second instance."

After a lengthy scroll through sped-up footage, something finally captured Ashley's eye.

"Wait," she said, her attention piqued.

"What?" Tim asked, eager to hear. Whenever his partner sounded like she had a light bulb moment, things usually got at least a little bit more interesting.

"Can we go back to that first fortnight, and just look through the daylight hours?" asked Ashley as she felt her pulse speed up.

When they began working through each day, Ashley pointed at the screen.

"This guy," she said. "I want to see just how often he's sitting there, not too far from the tiger enclosure."

As they indulged in working through two fortnight-long periods of footage, both agents observed the area around the enclosure - and the person who'd captured their attention.

"He's not quite right at the tiger enclosure, but you're right," said Tim. "He's close enough, and he is there a lot."

"Pretty much every single day," Ashley agreed. "And look at how intently he's always watching that tiger, even from that distance."

"True. Well, his uniform tells us that he works at the park," Tim added, nodding. "Looks like he's also watching the tiger most days. Could be someone of interest. Worth chatting to?"

"Yeah!" said Ashley. "Let's go."

"Now?" Tim asked, amused at her enthusiasm.

"Yeah, of course," Ashley replied. "It's only one. The park's open for another few hours yet. Come on."

Back at the park, they were instantly granted access through the main gate. Once inside, they began making their way through the park pathways again.

"Go back to talk to Michael Sanchez? See what he knows about the guy we saw on video?" Ashley asked.

"I don't think we're going to need to," Tim replied as he pointed down a side path. "Isn't that the person we're looking for?"

As Ashley looked in the direction that Tim was pointing, she saw the guy they'd been hoping to find. When he appeared to notice them, both agents saw him stand and quickly begin to walk in the opposite direction.

"Interesting," Tim muttered as he and Ashley both began walking briskly in the direction that the man had gone.

"Excuse me!" Ashley called out when she got closer.

While it seemed, for a moment, that the man was going to break out into a run, he then appeared to consider his options and instead slowly turned to face them.

"Mr. …?" Tim asked.

"Yenigun," the man replied slowly. "Who are you, and why are you chasing me?"

"We're Special Agents Power and Moore," Tim said as he showed his identification. "We'd like to ask you about your interest in the park's tiger."

Ashley watched the man start to look confused, as if that was the last thing he'd expected anyone to ask him about.

"Tigger?" he asked. "Has something happened to him?"

"He escaped," Tim said, not considering he should probably have provided a timeline for reference.

"He's gone?" the man asked, appearing distraught. "No, I was just outside his cage. He can't be gone."

"No, sorry. We mean that he has escaped over the past six months," Ashley said. "Twice."

"Oh. Yes, I know," the man said, visibly relieved. "But he's back and he's safe now."

"*He's* safe?" Tim asked. "He went to the home of a family."

"People want to hurt him," the man said. "I don't want them to."

As Ashley listened to the man speak, she began to think that they'd made an error in judgment.

"Sorry, Mr. Yenigun," she said and was immediately cut off by the man speaking.

"Chris," he said. "My name is Chris Yenigun."

"Yes, thank you, Chris," said Ashley. "We are here to find out how Tigger got out on those nights. We couldn't help but notice that you pay a lot of attention to him."

"He's my friend," Chris said as if that was the most logical explanation for everything the agents wanted to ask about.

Tim looked at Ashley. Although before them stood a mature adult, they could see clues that he was less mature in his mental growth.

"Then I believe you may be just the right person for us to talk to. Can you tell us more about Tigger?" Ashley asked and took time to listen to

Chris tell them in-depth about what he knew about the beautiful animal.

"I sit and eat my lunch with him almost every day," Chris continued to say.

"Yes," said Tim. "Why do you do that?"

"Because he's my friend," Chris said again, furrowing his brow in what seemed to be emotion bordering on annoyance that the agents just didn't get it.

"Do you know anything about the times when he escaped, Chris?" Ashley asked him. "You seem to know a lot about Tigger. What do you know about either or both of those nights?"

"*I* didn't seem him escape," Chris replied.

"No, of course not. Tell us, what exactly do you do in the park?" asked Tim.

"I clean out the enclosures of the aviary," said Chris.

"No night work then?"

"No, no night work for me," Chris said. "I come here at 10 am and leave at 4 pm, Saturday to Wednesday. That's when I work, but sometimes I come in on my days off just to see that Tigger is okay too."

"And you haven't heard anything about who might have taken Tigger?" Tim asked, observing the reaction that Chris had to the question.

"Taken? No, he escaped. That's what everyone said. I told them they were wrong, but nobody believes me," Chris said, seeming to grow a little more animated than he had been moments earlier. "He doesn't like being in a cage. That's not where he's meant to be. He always wants out. I can see it by the way he paces back and forth behind the wire. It's like a prison for him, but he has to live here."

"But how do you think he got out, Chris?" Ashley asked. "You seem to be someone who knows a lot about how things work with Tigger. Do you have a theory about how he came to escape?"

Both agents watched as the man appeared to grow increasingly uncomfortable. While a couple of minutes passed by, Ashley could see that the man was shutting down on them. Normally, she knew she would put a little bit of pressure on in her questioning. In the current circumstance, with the person they were talking to, she suspected pressure was only going to distress him more.

"You haven't seen anyone around who looks like they don't belong near the enclosure?" Tim asked, hoping to get some kind of useful information out of the guy.

"There's always lots of people," said Chris. "Every day, too many people. Tigger doesn't like them. He doesn't want to be around crowds anymore."

"Hmm," said Tim, resolved that there was nothing to learn from the park attendant. While the man in front of them certainly sounded passionate in talking about the tiger, he also sounded like his interest in it wasn't going to prove useful at all.

"Okay, well, thank you, Chris," Ashley said. "You have been very helpful."

As both agents prepared to walk away, Chris called out to them an afterthought.

"He wouldn't go by himself," he said. When Ashley and Tim turned to look at him, wondering what he meant, he said it again. "Tigger ... he wouldn't leave this place alone."

"Why would you say that?" Tim asked. "He's a wild animal..."

"No," said Chris. "He's been here since he was a cub. This is his home. He doesn't like the crowds, and he does want to be away from them, but he also knows that this is home."

"But you just said that he doesn't want to be here, and if there was a way … if a gate was open…"

"No!" Chris said, sounding frustrated. "I've seen him when the gate opens for the keepers to go in. He never tries to get out, even when awake and he could. *Never!*"

"Okay. Thank you," Ashley said when she read that Chris wasn't going to say anything more. "Keepers?" she asked, thinking about his wording before he started to walk away. When she saw him look confused, she expanded on her line of thought and questioning. "You said keepers, as in more than one? We met Wayne Medici. Is there another keeper for Tigger?"

"Three," said Chris. "Tigger has three keepers. They all work different days and nights."

Tim glanced at Ashley in recognition that not only had someone forgotten to tell them that, but they also hadn't noticed any different keepers in the footage they'd scrolled through.

"I see. Are you able to tell us their names?" Ashley asked.

Once again, Chris appeared to grow panicked. Ashley gave him a couple of minutes to answer before she made the decision to ease off and take that particular question elsewhere.

"That's okay," she said. "We don't need that information. Thanks again, Chris. You've been a great help. Tigger is lucky to have you as his friend."

"Why do you think nobody said that there were

more tiger keepers?" Ashley asked Tim as the two of them walked away.

"I'm guessing because we didn't ask," said Tim. "But I think the reason for that was because the owner, David Simpson, directed us straight away to Wayne Medici. Neither of them mentioned that there were more keepers for Tigger."

"And why would that be, I wonder," Ashley said as she considered that very question. "And also, how did the other keepers manage to not have their faces on those security footage files? That in itself makes me think they've got something to hide."

"Best we go and find out," said Tim, following Ashley as she was already heading down the path.

An hour later, the agents were once again walking out of the park. They'd gained the names of two other keepers who looked after Tigger on a rotation basis. The demeanor of the people who'd provided the names had indicated to Ashley and Tim that there probably hadn't been any intentional withholding of information, but rather an oversight. While both agents resolved to thoroughly check the backgrounds of the park staff, including the two new names, they equally felt that nothing was going to be found that would link to the case.

"Interesting afternoon," Tim said when they were driving back to the hotel again. "What's your gut feeling about Chris Yenigun? He seems obsessed with the tiger."

"Yeah, but I think that's a mental age or mental health thing," said Ashley. "We can't rule him and his obsession out, I guess, but I don't think he'd do anything to hurt Tigger, and I think he does see Tigger being elsewhere as something that would hurt."

"True. When he was speaking, it was hard to know if he agreed with Tigger being locked in that enclosure or not. He started saying that Tigger wanted to be free and away from the crowds," said Tim, remembering the conversation. "He also said that Tigger wouldn't escape even if he could, which was interesting. Actually, I think he said he didn't think Tigger would escape even if he could and he was *awake*."

"Yeah, I heard that too," said Ashley, nodding. "Weird choice of words."

"Unless he does know something," said Tim.

"And Tigger was taken out … asleep?" Ashley pondered. "But by who? Who could do that?"

Tim turned and looked at her.

"A vet," he said before pulling out his phone, making a quick call, and smiling at Ashley. "Greg Samson from Sunny Vets."

"GPS it," Ashley said, nodding toward the unit on the dashboard. "A vet practice will probably be shut now, but let's pay them a visit in the morning."

# CHAPTER 8

"So what are we thinking we need to find out from this vet?" Tim asked when they were having breakfast the following morning. "I'm guessing he has the ability to put Tigger into a deep sleep, which could prove to be a vital part of whatever happened on those two occasions."

"Yep, and he was the one who retrieved the tiger from the Templeton home and got it safely back to the park," said Ashley. "That, at least, proves that he's familiar with how to safely transport Tigger from one location to another as well."

"That kind of sounds like a theory that Tigger didn't just walk out of the wildlife park and make his way to the Templeton property," said Tim. "If we go with that, it definitely looks like an intended event."

"Yeah, I think we're both in agreement that it would have to have been an intended and organized event, aren't we?" Ashley asked and saw him nod. "While it's not impossible that Tigger did that not once but twice, it just seems very unlikely. But hey, maybe this vet - Greg Samson - will enlighten us to something about tigers that will make us view this differently."

"True," said Tim. "It's quite interesting really, isn't it. First time I've worked on a case involving an animal. We might be tiger professionals by the time we finish this one," he added, making Ashley laugh.

"You reckon," she said, not bothering to make it a question. "But back to your question - what do we need to find out from the vet? Well, he was the one who got Tigger back. However he did that is important. I have no idea how a creature that large is moved, whether awake or asleep. Maybe learning just about that will help us."

"True," Tim agreed. "Ready to go?"

Sitting in the veterinary practice waiting room twenty minutes later, Ashley and Tim quietly watched the coming and going of staff and pet owners. When there was a gap in the flow, and the waiting room was empty of further visitors, the receptionist finally called them over to her.

"I'll take you through to see Mr. Samson now," she said before leading them down the corridor.

When Ashley and Tim entered the small office they'd been directed to, they were faced by a man who looked to be in his late thirties. Although he stood and held out his hand to them, it was easy for both agents to see that he was nervous.

"How … how can I help you, Agents?" he asked after their introductions.

"We would like to talk to you about the tiger at the wildlife park in town," Tim said.

"Tigger," Greg Samson said with what looked like a mild attempt at producing a smile. "Quite a specimen, and definitely not a type of creature I have a lot of experience working with."

"But you *do* work with him?" Ashley asked.

"On occasion, I have," Greg answered. "As for all of the animals up there, I am the person who completes their health checks or required surgeries, and administers any jabs they need, but it's only a few days a year that I'd be there." He paused and waited for any questions to be produced. "May I ask what brings you here today? Has something happened with Tigger?"

"As you know, he got out..." Tim said quietly.

"Yes, of course," Greg said. "Everyone in town knows about that misfortune."

"*Two* misfortunes," Tim added to see if he could prompt the discomfort level of the vet to go up a notch. It took little effort. Straight away, the man in front of him began to fidget in discomfort.

"What can you tell us about those instances when he escaped?" Ashley asked, confident that Tim would be doing his people-reading thing. It was one of the reasons he was such a good agent. His gut instinct was close to being right almost all the time when it came to figuring people out.

"I was called to tranquilize him so he could be transported back to the park," Greg said.

Ashley watched his face as he provided the brief summary. There was no hiding the degree to which he gulped before and after he spoke.

"You'd done that before those occasions?" she asked. "Tranquilize Tigger, I mean."

"Several times," said Greg. "He's had the occasional injury, and a tooth pulled out about a year ago. Anything like that, it's easiest to put him under to carry a procedure out."

"Right. And speaking of carrying, how much would a tiger weigh?" Tim asked.

"A lot," Greg replied.

"One person couldn't carry him?"

"No," Greg said. "Well, there would be no possible way for an *average* person to carry him. He's still quite young, so not anywhere as large as tigers do grow to, but he's certainly big enough to present a challenge. I guess, like anything, *someone* out there might be able to lift a weight like that."

"Not you, though," Tim asked.

For a long while, the vet looked at Tim as he remained silent before shifting his view to Ashley and then back again.

"I can't say that I've ever *tried* to lift Tigger by myself, but I'd have to say that I *assume* I wouldn't be able to lift him alone, no," Greg finally said. "Look, what is this really about?"

"We are just trying to figure out what happened," Ashley said.

"A wild animal escaped its confinement and made its way through our town," said Greg. "Sorry, but I'm at a loss to understand why this would gain the attention of your organization, or why you're questioning *me* about it."

"You don't know anything more about the instance?" Ashley asked.

"Like what?"

"Like … how or why a tiger *would* get out of that park, and if he did, why he wouldn't attack anyone and everyone in his path," Ashley said. "Is he wild or is he tame?"

"As far as I know, that tiger has been up there pretty much all of his life," Greg said. "Does that make him tame? Maybe, compared to his fully wild counterparts, it does to a small degree. He's certainly used to being around humans, but don't think that he's just like an oversized household cat. He is a wild animal. It's in his makeup, and it's his instinct to do as any other tiger in the world would do."

Hearing the tone of the vet change from an attempt at being friendly, to growing highly agitated, Ashley decided to call the questioning short. Sometimes, it was questioning that got the answers they wanted. Sometimes, a better way to get answers was to back right off and then watch to see what the person did *after* Ashley and Tim had left.

"Yes. Well, I'm sure you have much work to get on with so we won't hold you up any longer, but just one more question, Mr. Samson," Ashley said. "If this tiger didn't walk the distance that it did, how could someone have transported him?"

"You … you think that someone took him to that house?" Greg replied with a slight stutter in his delivery of the question.

"It's a possibility, isn't it?" asked Tim, curious about the vet's body language changing as much as it did when Ashley had asked her last question.

"Not everyone could handle a tiger," Greg answered, his voice in almost a whisper.

"No, I'm sure they couldn't," said Ashley. "But please enlighten me. Could Tigger, for example, fit into a small truck or a car?"

After watching the vet clear his throat, she heard his answer.

"A small truck - yes, definitely," he said. "A car - yes, maybe, if it was a large car."

"Alright, well, thank you," she said, standing. "I think you've answered all the questions we have for the moment."

Although Tim was a little perplexed about the briefness of the meeting, he followed her out without questioning why. She knew her reason. He knew that whatever that turned out to be, her instinct would pay off.

# CHAPTER 9

"You think he's our guy?" Tim asked Ashley when they were on the road again. "Certainly seems suspicious."

"Yeah, he's definitely hiding something, but what could his motive be?" Ashley asked. "He's a vet. The Templetons don't have any pets that we know of. How would their paths even have crossed?"

"I don't know, but it's not a huge city. It's not beyond possibility that their paths just happened to cross sometime," said Tim, just as his mobile alerted him to a call coming in. After a brief phone conversation, he turned and looked at Ashley. "That was Sarah. The computer forensics team have finished assessing the park footage."

"And?" Ashley asked.

"It has been doctored," Tim replied. "They said a good job's been done on it - far too good for an amateur - but someone has worked to cover up something."

"Okay. Did she say *how* it's been manipulated? Was some of it cut out - like the center part when Tigger would have left the enclosure?"

"Yes and no. It was the mostly date of the footage that was changed," said Tim. "That footage of Tigger going into his cage that night, and then the footage of through the night, was actually filmed ten months ago. The only bit that was real on either file for those nights was when we saw Tigger being returned to his enclosure after his capture."

"Hmm," Ashley replied. "I think we need to go and talk to the Templetons again, but first, let's head back to the hotel and you can do your thing in searching for anything about Greg Samson. Maybe there's something in his past that will be of interest to us."

When back in the hotel room, Tim began using his system access to see if they could find anything out about the vet that they hadn't already.

"He's not in the system," he said after searching. "He also doesn't have any social media, which is strange if he's computer-savvy enough to be able to change those security footage files."

"In my opinion, not all criminals would want to be seen on the Internet," Ashley said, smiling. "But if it *was* Greg Samson who doctored the security recordings, we need to ask how he got in to change that footage. Did he make his way into the park somehow and do it at that location? How could he have gotten in with all those locked gates?"

"Even if he does frequent the park far more often than he let on, it doesn't seem likely that he'd have keys for those gates," said Tim. "And if he doesn't have a way to freely get in and out of the park, how could he have gotten in there at all to release Tigger, let alone get into the security office to alter the footage?"

"And what could possibly be his motive?" Ashley asked again. "Neither Mr. or Mrs. Templeton work in jobs related to animals…"

"Unless there's a connection between him and Alana Templeton," said Tim.

"Work related?" Ashley asked out loud. "Or

something else altogether?"

"Affair?" asked Tim, shrugging his shoulders. "Like I said before, they live in the same town. The idea of them meeting isn't impossible."

"Less likely that it's the love interest that gets attacked or killed, though," said Ashley, pondering the option. "More likely that it would have been Steven to be attacked in that instance."

"Maybe … unless Greg had feelings for Alana and she didn't reciprocate them," said Greg. "We've seen plenty of situations where that particular type of situation changed someone from being normal, to being something completely different."

"Agreed. Yeah, I think we need to go and talk to the Templetons again," Ashley said, standing up. "Let's go."

Tim followed suit as he silently agreed with what Ashley had just said. The Templetons had initially presented themselves as a traumatized family who were innocent, but there were far too many questions to be asked, and far too many possibilities that had to be ruled out. Also still under consideration were the demeanors of both Alana and Steven Templeton during their first meeting with Ashley and Tim. Neither agent had forgotten just how vague both people had seemed.

# CHAPTER 10

"Mrs. Templeton, we'd like to ask you some more questions, if that's okay with you," Tim said when they were greeted at the front door of the residence.

"Oh, yes, of course," Alana Templeton replied as she shifted her toddler, Tony, from one hip to the other. "I do need to head out to an appointment in a few minutes, but please … come in."

"Thank you," Ashley said. "We won't hold you up for long."

"Have you found something out?" Alana asked when she sat down and watched the agents do the same on the sofa facing her. "Was … was this intentional? The tiger showing up here, I mean."

"We are still investigating, Mrs. Templeton," said Tim.

"Oh, please, just call me Alana."

"Alana," Tim acknowledged before continuing. "We have some names that we'd like to run past you, just to make sure none of these people are someone who…"

"Might hate me?" Alana asked before Tim had time to finish his question.

"We are investigating all options, Alana," Ashley said. "Can I read some names out to you?" she asked, observing the wriggling infant in Alana's arms.

"Yes, of course," Alana replied. "What … who are they?"

As Ashley began reading out names of the people who'd caught her attention at the wildlife park, she and Tim watched Alana's face. When one name had been read out, in particular, they both saw her frown.

"You know someone on this list?" Tim asked, trying to dispel his random hypothesis that Alana and the vet, Greg Samson, might know each other intimately. That scenario would have been a long-shot, but certainly not impossible.

"Medici…" Alana said as she focused on the surname.

"Wayne Medici?" Ashley asked, curious.

"Hmm … Medici…" Alana said again, appearing to have to push her mind to concentrate. "No. Nick!" she finally said. "Yes - Nick!"

"Nick … Medici?" asked Tim and saw her nod.

"Yes," said Alana. "I represented Nick Medici, but that was a few years back. Sorry, the name sounded so familiar, but no, not the one you mentioned."

"Right, but is Nick a relation of Wayne, do you know?" Ashley asked.

"It's possible," said Alana, nodding while shrugging her shoulders in a way that looked far more casual than her tone sounded. "I know that there were a few of them here in town, and they were related, but I really couldn't say."

"What was the charge that Nick was on when you represented him, if I may ask?" asked Tim.

"Oh, Nick Medici was put away for selling drugs," Alana answered.

"Put away?" Tim asked and saw her nod. "And you were his defense?" he further asked and saw her nod again.

"Yes, I fought for him, but the prosecution had so much evidence against him," Alana said. "To be honest, it would have been only sheer luck if I'd managed to keep him *out* of prison, with all that they had on him."

Tim and Ashley looked at one another. A disgruntled family member of someone who'd been put in prison? It was a motive they'd seen quite a few times in their careers.

"Aren't you supposed to be on your way to your appointment, Honey?" they heard Steven Templeton ask as he walked into the room. The look of surprise and then nervousness on his face as he noticed the agents wasn't lost on Ashley or Tim.

"Oh, gosh, yes!" Alana said, standing abruptly. "I'm so sorry. It's a medical appointment that I really can't miss, but I'll be home by five if we need to continue this…"

"No, that is fine, Mrs. Templeton," Tim said, standing. "What you've given us is enough to go on with for the moment."

Ashley and Tim remained where they were as they watched the changeover of infant from one parent to the other, and then saw Alana run out toward the door. When she was gone, Steven Templeton approached them.

"I think the stress of all this is starting to get to my wife," he said. "She … she isn't her usual self, I'm afraid."

"That's very understandable, Mr. Templeton," Ashley said, watching his face. She thought he had an odd tone in his voice. As she studied him, she wondered if he was on edge, or he was just like that all the time. "I know we asked you this previously, but is there anyone you can think of who would want to hurt you?"

"No," Steven replied, shaking his head. "I'm a surgeon. It's my job to save people. I'm not in the habit of *hurting* them."

"I'm sure, but it can take any small thing to set someone off," said Tim. "No ghosts in your closet … so to speak?"

Both agents watched as Steven Templeton appeared to contemplate how to answer. After a long moment of silence, Tim pushed a little harder.

"You're not having an affair?" he asked. When he saw a look of panic on the face of the man in front of him, he quickly worked to tone down the question. "We wouldn't be judging you if you are," he said. "We're just trying to uncover who might have reason to want to do this to you and your family."

"Who might have reason to put a *tiger* in our yard?" Steven asked. "I mean, that would take someone pretty fucked up (excuse my language)."

"You haven't answered the question, Mr. Templeton," Ashley said, her tone serious. "*Is* there another woman in your life?"

After a long while, Steven finally revealed the truth.

"Now? No," he said. "But I did have an affair a long time ago."

"I see," said Tim. "Can you tell us who that was with?"

"Nobody," said Steven. "I mean, I haven't seen or heard from her since I broke it off with her three years ago. Alana and I had been going through a period of … unhappiness, I guess. I met this woman, Rey, and she was just like that - a ray of sunshine. I guess we just met at that moment when I needed someone to help me feel good ... to help me feel *alive*."

"And how long were you seeing her for?" asked Ashley.

"Almost two years," said Steven. "There was a time when I considered leaving Alana and going to give things a real go with Rey. Then things started to turn around here. Alana fell pregnant with this little one and ... I dunno ... everything seemed to change."

"Change how?" asked Tim.

"I just ... I guess I'd needed to be reminded of how amazing my wife is, and how good we've got it," said Steven. "The combination of Alana and I finding our way back to one another again, and Tony being born, just seemed to ... realign us again."

"So when Tony came along, you broke things off with this other woman?" Tim asked.

"Yes," Steven said. "As soon as I knew I needed to stop running away from the unhappiness I'd been feeling here, and start focusing on Alana and the kids again, I told Rey that it was over."

"And how did she react?" Tim asked.

"She reacted remarkably well, considering," said Steven. "We'd always said it was a good time for both of us, and we'd make sure to enjoy it for however long it lasted. When I knew I had to focus on Alana and the kids, I told Rey that I was going to stop seeing her. She smiled and wished me well. Like I said, I haven't seen or heard from her since."

"Not even a phone call, or a text message?" asked Ashley.

"No phone call. No texts. Absolutely nothing," said Steven.

"And does your wife know about the affair?" Ashley asked, curious to hear the answer.

"No," Steven replied, his head lowering slightly as he looked down at the ground. "I always meant to tell her, but couldn't bring myself to. I will eventually, but things are too good between us now, and she's happy - most of the time, anyway. I don't want to hurt her. Maybe when the kids are a bit older, I'll take the chance and tell her everything. Right now, I just want us to keep moving forward as we have been since that happened," he said looking at the agents again. "I love my wife and my kids. I did something stupid, but it was a long time ago. I'm not doing that again."

Ashley nodded. Although he might not deserve any 'husband of the year' award, she was confident she was seeing true regret on his face.

"And there's nobody who you think would want to hurt you or Alana?" she asked. "Not through your work?"

"No, I don't think so," he said. "Like I said, I'm a surgeon. Not all operations go well, or go to plan. Sometimes, people's families are left grieving, but I've never been threatened by anyone. There's no particular case that I can think of where I met anyone who looked like they wanted to cause me or any of the hospital staff any harm." He paused as he looked at both agents, thoughtful. "You agree with my suspicion that this was intentional?"

"Well, this is a unique situation. It being intentional is certainly not something we can rule out just yet," Ashley replied.

"So … but then … that means … it could happen *again?*" Steven asked.

"We're still investigating, Mr. Templeton," said

Tim. "But we are confident that we're going to find out how this happened to your family, and who's behind it."

Both agents remained silent for a long while, watching Steven Templeton's face and wondering if he was going to present them with any further information or any questions he might have. When he seemed to not want to offer either, Tim and Ashley looked at one another before refocusing on the man in front of them.

"We'll leave you now," Ashley said. "Please do call us if anything more happens, or if you think of anything else."

"Yes, I will do that," Steven said, standing to walk the agents out. "Thank you."

"I don't think I like him," Tim said as they made their way back to the car. "I don't know why. He's just one of those … really … *unlikable* people."

Ashley smiled at him when they were settled in their seats.

"I do know what you mean," she said. "Still, at least he was forthcoming about the affair he had. It certainly makes our job a little easier when they come clean about things like that."

"True. We haven't put the same question to his wife," Tim said, thinking out loud. "About whether she's having an affair, I mean."

"Yeah, but if you're still thinking that she might know Greg Samson, maybe we could put more pressure on him," said Ashley. "He seems to either know something more than he's shared with us, or he's afraid of something."

"I do think we should delve deeper into Samson's background and movements," Tim said. "I got as far as seeing that he had no social media and no criminal record, but when we were with him, I kept getting the feeling that there is a lot more to him than we've found out yet."

"Alright, let's do that in the morning."

# CHAPTER 11

"Think we'll find out anything different today?" Tim asked the following morning as they made their way to the veterinary clinic again.

"I agree that, during our last meeting with him, Samson seemed too nervous to ignore," Ashley replied. "Let's just have another chat with him and see what he says this time. If you have a theory that he might know Alana Templeton, let's ask him straight out if he does. Even if he denies it, I'm confident you'll be able to tell if he's lying."

Inside the clinic, they once again waited for a break in the customer queue before they were shown into Greg Samson's office again.

"I thought I answered all your questions yesterday," he said to the agents when they were seated and he'd closed his office door. "Have you made some progress on your investigation?"

"We mainly want to ask you about your relationship with the Templetons," Tim said as he prepared to closely observe the vet's facial expression.

As Ashley and Tim both watched, they were surprised to see Greg Samson grow visibly uneasy, almost to the point where he looked like he was starting to sweat. Rather than say or ask anything at that moment, both agents remained quiet and waited. Eventually, their wait came to an end as the vet looked at each of them and spoke.

"I want protection for my family," he said, fear clearly evident in his voice.

"I'm not sure..." Ashley started to say. Her sentence was cut short by the vet speaking again, this time with enhanced panic in his voice.

"I can share something with you, but I want - *need* - protection for my family!" he said with force.

"We can certainly look at arranging something like that for you," said Tim. "But we need to understand why you're asking for it first. Why don't you tell us what you know."

"I ... I was threatened," Greg started to say. "They said that if I didn't do what they wanted, they would kill every member of my family."

"Who? Do you know who it was that threatened you?" asked Ashley.

"No, I don't know who they are," said Greg. "All I knew was that it was up to me to tranquilize the tiger and help get it to that address."

"Okay. Can you tell us the whole story from start to end?" Tim asked. "If you want us to help your family, you're going to have to help us better understand what's happened and how this all came about."

"Yes. I ... I received a threat, like I said," Greg said. "They were so specific with the details they told about my family, and they said to not tell anyone. The things they said they'd do to my kids..."

As Tim and Ashley watched, they saw the man in front of them begin to grow highly emotional. He also exhibited the same mannerisms they'd observed in many other cases - the mannerism of finally letting out something that he'd been holding in and telling nobody about.

"All I had to do was put the tiger to sleep and help load him into a pickup that came to the park," he said. "If I did that, they said they'd leave my family alone."

"Okay, and who decided where the tiger would be taken to?" Ashley asked.

"They did. I don't know who they are, and I didn't know where we were taking Tigger. I swear!" Greg continued. "I was told that a guy would have the pickup, and the access to the park. He was also the one who knew where we had to go and drop the tiger off. It was my job to handle the slow wake-up of Tigger on the property so that he'd wake up close to the house just after sunrise." Before them, he began to break down, appearing unsuccessfully to try to hold back tears before he continued. "I didn't know what it was all for. I didn't know it was going to be taken to someone's *home*..."

"So you don't know the Templetons?" Tim asked. "Alana Templeton, or Steven Templeton?"

"No," said Greg, shaking his head. "I'd never been to the house before..."

"Before ... that first time, or the second?" asked Ashley.

"No, just this time," Greg said in almost a whisper. "I don't know anything about the previous time that the tiger got out."

"Okay," Tim said. "And the person who helped you to transport the tiger - who was that?"

"I don't know," said Greg, shrugging. "I was only told that a guy would be at the gate, would get me in, would help me load the sleeping tiger into the vehicle, and then he'd drive a route that would avoid any street cameras. Once we were there, and the tiger was in the very first stages of starting to wake up, he dropped me back at the park so I could get my car and be gone before any staff got there. I haven't seen the guy since."

"You don't know even his first name?" Ashley asked. "If you can, please tell us anything that you know about this person, that could help us to find him and hopefully corroborate your story."

"I … maybe … Len? Lennie? Liam? I don't know. L-*something*," Greg said. "Briefly mentioned that he was a computer geek, and said in passing that he had something to do with how we weren't going to get caught. Something to do with the cameras. I didn't ask what he meant. I didn't want to ask anything. I didn't want to *know* anything."

Ashley nodded at him as she processed what he was saying. The open distress he exhibited was good. It gave Ashley hope that he was possibly telling the truth. What he could be charged with for his part in whatever had panned out, she wasn't interested in at that moment. She knew their main focus had to be finding the other person who'd helped with the tiger escaping and getting to the Templeton home. Once they found that person, just maybe they would also find out who was behind the odd crime - and why.

"My family?" Greg asked again, pleading evident in his voice. "If they find out I've talked to you, my family… my *children*…"

"We're going to see what we can do about that," Ashley said. There was no way of gauging who they were ultimately going to be dealing with, or what they were capable of. Regardless, if there was any chance that any child was going to be hurt, she would do whatever she could to prevent that from happening. "We'll leave you now, but we will be in touch again soon. For the moment, there won't be any reason why someone should know you've talked to us. We can keep that information to ourselves - for the moment, at least," she added before she and Tim stood and walked out.

An hour later, Tim received a call from the computer forensics team member who'd been studying the security footage of the park. After listening to the details that had been revealed to him, he turned to face Ashley.

"We've got an address ... and a name," Tim said.

"For?" Ashley asked.

"For the guy that altered the security footage at the wildlife park," Tim replied. "Liam Manson."

"Ahh! That's the 'L-something' we're seeking then, I'm guessing," she said and saw Tim nod. "That gives some credence to what Greg Samson told us. I don't suppose the team also figured out how he got into the park to make the changes to the footage?"

"He didn't," said Tim. "He hacked in from what the guys think might be his home. This is the address they gave me," he continued before entering the address into the dash GPS unit.

Without saying a word, Ashley happily planted her foot on the accelerator. Sometimes, it was slow going, figuring anything out, but as they advanced each step and got closer to what they were trying to find out, her excitement always went up a notch.

On the way to the address they'd been provided with, Tim pulled out his laptop and logged into the system to find out whatever he could about Liam Manson.

"This guy's got quite a bit of a rap sheet," Tim informed Ashley as she drove.

"Not from helping tigers to harass families, I take it," Ashley surmised.

"No," Tim replied, chuckling quietly. "He's in the system because of the huge amount of hacking he's been doing since he was twelve."

"*Twelve?!*" exclaimed Ashley. "Geez, what kinds of places has he been charged with hacking into?"

"You name it - looks like he's tried it," said Tim. "A heap of online businesses mainly. Seems like he's been using his skills to place orders for things without paying for them, mostly, by the look of it."

"Nothing too nefarious then," Ashley said, intrigued.

"He's broken the law and been charged fifteen times, Ash," Tim said, surprised by her reaction.

"Well, yeah, but has he used his skills to facilitate the hurting of anyone, or to play havoc with any big systems - electricity grid or banks?" Ashley asked.

"No, not that he's been charged with," said Tim. "I do get what you're saying. His charges look like he's mostly just been a kid who realized he could get stuff for free if he figured out how. That doesn't, however, negate that he's broken the law."

"Agreed," Ashley said, turning and smiling at him. "What else do we need to know before we talk to this guy?"

"That's all that I can see on his record," Tim answered.

"Okay, and how old is he now?" Ashley asked.

"Twenty-two," Tim said. "More than old enough to now know and fully understand about the law and about consequences."

"True. Looks like it's just up here," Ashley said as they made the turn into the street they'd been provided with.

"Let's hope Liam Manson can provide us with another piece of this puzzle," said Tim, wondering yet again how everything was going to fit together to make the very odd puzzle complete.

# CHAPTER 12

Pulling up to the address they'd gained for Liam Manson, Ashley felt nervous. They'd left behind what had appeared to be a fairly safe area of town. Where they currently were looked more like a war zone - or a neighborhood that had suffered from years of being caught up in gang rivalry.

After readying themselves for anything that might happen, the two agents began to walk to the door of the modest and run-down bungalow. Although it looked almost derelict, Ashley could see signs of it being currently lived in.

"What do you want?" Tim and Ashley heard from a man who'd appeared from down the side of the house.

"Mr. Manson?" Ashley asked, noticing the guy's nervousness. For a moment, she suspected from his facial expression that he was going to bolt. Another moment longer, he seemed to consider his options and instead moved closer to where she stood with Tim.

"What's this about?" he asked, his voice noticeably quiet.

"We're Special Agents Moore and…"

"Yeah, yeah, I can see what you are," Liam said. "Just tell me what you're here for."

Tim watched the face of the man in front of them. It was rare that a criminal stood their ground and faced him and Ashley so peacefully when they'd done something wrong - or even when they hadn't, in some cases.

"We're investigating the escape of a tiger from the wildlife park in town," Tim said, monitoring the man's expression as he spoke. "We believe you know something about that."

After a lengthy period of silence and what appeared to be much contemplation, Liam spoke again, this time in almost a whisper.

"Look," he said quietly. "Inside that house is my fiancée, who is seven months pregnant. That tiger job, I would have never taken on, but they threatened to kill not only my woman, but also my unborn baby. My *unborn baby*! When I received the threat, I … I couldn't go to the cops. I'm sure you already know I've been in trouble with them plenty of times before. They wouldn't have helped me. I didn't have any choice. To save my kid, I needed to do what they wanted."

"They, who?" Ashley asked. "Liam, who is behind this?"

Both agents watched as Liam Manson grew more fidgety and alert, looking around him as if he thought someone else might be watching him.

"Baby, who is that?" they all heard a woman's voice call out from behind a screen door at the front of the house.

"Nobody, Baby," Liam called back, smiling and waving. "Nothing for you to worry about. I'll be inside in a minute." He watched the door until she could be seen no longer, and then turned back to the agents. "She doesn't know about any of this, and I don't want her to. She's been pregnant before and … and I'll protect her and my baby this time, no matter what it takes."

Ashley nodded, somewhat surprised by the level of passion and protectiveness that the young man showed.

"Well, we do need to talk to you," said Tim. "If you don't want to have this conversation here and now, tell us where and when."

"Yeah, I need to help her with something, and I'll make her some lunch. She likes that part of the day," Liam said. "I do need to go out later to get some more stuff from the supermarket. I can meet you in the carpark there at two."

Although neither agent suspected he'd follow through with that plan, something about Liam made them want to at least give him a chance to do the right thing.

"Two then," Tim said. "If you're not there, we'll be back here…"

"I'll *be* there!" Liam insisted before turning and walking inside.

Once back in the car, Ashley turned to face Tim.

"Think he'll turn up? Or should we stay around here and watch his movements just in case he's planning to get out of town?" she asked.

"I actually think there's a chance he's going to follow through," said Tim. "Nothing's ever guaranteed with these guys, but he looked genuinely spooked and worried about his fiancée and unborn baby. That might be enough for him to make a wise choice."

"Okay," said Ashley as she glanced at her watch. "We've got some time to kill, then. Lunch?" she asked, smiling at him. During any investigation, there was always a moment of teasing to be had when it came to Tim's appetite.

"Thought you'd never ask," Tim said, grinning at

her.

Two hours later, the agents sat in the supermarket carpark, watching for Liam to appear. As the minutes passed and Ashley's watch showed 2:05 pm, she sighed.

"I was hopeful this one might be an easy one," she said just before she saw their person of interest walk out of the supermarket with a trolley full to the brim with groceries. "And there he is. Guess he was inside the whole time we were sitting here."

"Yeah," replied Tim. "Let's get the information we need before he takes off."

As they approached Liam, they saw him open the boot of his car and begin placing grocery bags inside of it.

"Look, I told you they threatened my woman and my kid," Liam said quietly as he slowly transferred each bag from the trolley into the boot. "I thought it was just a job of altering some security footage. I didn't know till the last minute that I was going to be helping some guy to move a giant fucking cat! By that stage, they had me so scared that I didn't feel I had any choice. I was there at the park, and they said they were sitting outside my house, ready to hurt my woman ... and my baby ... what else could I do?"

"That's understandable, Liam, but do you know who it was that was giving you these instructions?" Tim asked.

"Nope," said Liam. "The voice was definitely a guy's voice, but I didn't recognize it as anyone I knew."

"Do you have any suspicion about who it was? They must have known you to have had your phone number or address," said Ashley.

"I thought…" Liam said as he looked around in paranoia again, and then turned to face her. "A couple of months ago, I hacked into the power company database. I swear, all I wanted was to alter our bill so that we wouldn't have to pay so much. Things are so tight…"

"Sure. And?" asked Tim.

"When I was digging around in there, about to alter our bill, I noticed that something was off with it," Liam said. "When I look at data, sometimes I can see things - irregularities. It's like they just pop out at me, like a neon sign beginning to flash in front of my eyes. Anyway, when I looked closely at just our data, I could see that someone *else* had hacked into that system and had upped the bill total."

"You mean the power company had some kind of … price increase?" Tim asked.

"No, that's what caught my eye," said Liam. "Someone had lodged some code that pushed the customer power bills up by five per cent, and then that extra money was coded to be diverted to another account - someone's *private* bank account. Anyway, it caught my eye because that's the sort of thing that *I* do - not to affect anyone else; just to help out me and my girl financially, you know?"

Tim nodded, suspicious of the story they were being told, but also very intrigued.

"Go on," he insisted.

"Well, I wish I hadn't, but I kept digging," said Liam. "I know I should have stopped there. I didn't. Eventually, I could see who owned the bank account that the cash was going into, and I mean, it was a *lot* of money that they were accumulating. Five per cent on an electricity bill doesn't sound like much but this person was taking it from a *lot* of people. How they got away with it for so long, I have no idea. Highlighted to me how little some of the IT guys who work for these big companies know sometimes, you know?"

"And you think that this person who'd done this was the same person who contacted you to do the tiger job?" Ashley asked. "Why - and how - would you think that?"

"It was something they said when they first contacted me," said Liam. "I can't remember the exact wording of the conversation, but they said something in passing that made me click that they *knew* I'd found out about their code and what they were doing."

"But if they're a hacker too, able to facilitate what you're talking about, why would they even need you?" Tim asked. "Wouldn't they have just hacked into the camera footage and changed it themselves?"

"But that's just it - they're not a hacker," said Liam. "They're not even all that computer savvy. They - the chick who owns the bank account that the money was going into - she works at the power company. She's just an admin assistant."

"But you said it was a man who called you. And anyone who could do what you're talking about would have to have at least some kind of skill in computer programming or changing code to do that, wouldn't they?" asked Ashley.

"In a regular situation, yes, but when I'd studied it all for long enough, I could see the path of everything that had happened," Liam said as he placed the last bag in the boot and closed it. "The altering was done onsite in the company HQ, at her workstation. I think someone else might have *written* the code, but she's the one who uploaded it into the system directly through an external USB drive."

"Hmm," Tim said as he considered the likelihood of what they were being told was true. "Alright. Can you tell us the name of this person?"

"Some chick called Rayna - Rayna Cunningham," said Liam.

"And you don't know her?" Tim asked and saw Liam shake his head.

"Nope! Never heard of her before I dived a little too deep into all that," Liam replied.

"Sorry, Liam, please tell me if I'm correctly understanding what you're saying," said Ashley. "You hacked into the power company system, saw someone else had already been in there to set up a way for them to overcharge customers and then skim money from the company, and then … *they* saw *you* in there, so contacted you and threatened you?"

"I know it sounds farfetched but, yeah - pretty much," Liam said, nodding. "Like I said, it was a guy who called me to threaten me, but he referred to 'her' and 'she' a couple of times when he was speaking. I'm sure the two things are connected. Don't ask my why I think that. I just do. I don't know what that chick's deal was, or why she wanted the job done, but I'm 99% sure that she was the one behind the threats to me and my family."

"You believe she was the one who wanted the tiger taken?" Tim asked for clarification.

"Yeah," said Liam. "Like I say, don't ask me why. Fucking stupid plan, if you ask me. I mean, what was she hoping would happen?"

"Can you tell us what exactly the plan *was*?" Ashley asked. "You were contacted and told to … change the security footage of the cameras that night?"

"Yeah," Liam said, nodding. "It was gonna be my job to change the footage, so that whatever happened, it would look like *nothing* had happened. So I went back pretty far - ten or eleven months - and transferred the old footage to sit over the new footage, and changed the date so nobody would be able to see the tiger being taken out."

"Okay, and then what else?"

"As well as doing that, I was told that I had to go to a certain location on the road, out by the edge of the woods, and there would be a pickup waiting there with the keys in it," said Liam. "I did that, got the pickup, and went to the park. Inside the pickup were keys to get inside."

"And you met someone there to help you?" Ashley asked and saw him nod again.

"Yeah, a vet, I think," said Liam. "Don't know what his name was. We talked for a couple of minutes and then both decided we didn't want to know anything other than what we already knew."

"Okay, and then what happened next, after you met him at the park?"

"He did what he does, and played what seemed to be his part in it all - put the tiger to sleep - and then we loaded the thing onto the back of the pickup," said Liam. "After that was done, I received a message to take it to that address. When I saw that, I freaked. I mean, it's one thing to hack into a computer system. It's another to grab a wild animal. But putting something like that in a person's *home*? That's well and truly fucked up."

"But you did it," said Ashley.

"They were sitting outside my house, ready to do whatever they wanted to my girl and my baby!" Liam said with passion and panic in his voice. "Not only that, but when they contacted me, they knew things that they shouldn't have - things like the expected date of birth of my baby. The *exact date*! How did they know that? Only the hospital - or specifically, the doctor who my girl has been seeing for her appointments - should know that," he said and paused for a long while before speaking again. "I know … I *know* we could have gone to the cops or something, but at that moment, I knew I couldn't get home quick enough to protect her. I would have done anything to make sure she wasn't hurt. I didn't know for sure who the guy was - the vet. Was he part of the plan? I didn't know. I didn't trust anyone and I wasn't going to risk anything happening at home."

"And they knew that, obviously," Tim said. "Okay, so this Rayna Cunningham - did you hear from her directly, or from the guy who called with the instructions that night, *after* the job was done?"

"Neither, thank fuck," said Liam. "We did that job, and then I had to drop the vet in one place and then go back and drop the pickup off at the same place I'd picked it up. Made sure I wiped it down as best I could to make sure my prints weren't left on it. Then I went home and was relieved to see that my girl didn't seem to have known anything was wrong, or what threat she'd been under. I waited for something to happen after that, but nothing has. No word from them. No issue about anything. Even after I read in the paper about the tiger getting out and turning up at that house, I've heard nothing."

As Ashley and Tim processed all the details they'd received, they saw Liam look at them once again with pleading in his eyes.

"Look, I know that it's not cool hacking into systems and doing stupid crap like that," he said. "I'm trying to do better - I'm *going* to do better - but that night … I just didn't feel like there was any choice but to do what they wanted. I've got a baby due soon, and I'm trying to clean up my life…"

"Right now, Liam, our priority is finding out who's ultimately behind all of this," said Ashley. "But if we don't talk to you again, it *is* likely that someone else will. Don't leave town."

They watched as they saw Liam nod and walk to the driver side of his car. They didn't try and stop him. They knew where he lived. They also believed his sincerity about why he'd done what he'd done - at least for the moment. Before he climbed inside his vehicle, both agents noticed how defeated he looked. Nothing more was said as they turned to walk away, hoping he'd been telling the truth.

"Thoughts?" Ashley asked him when she started the car engine.

"Well, we've got another name," Tim said. "It's all starting to look like one elaborate plan that someone with not-normal thinking has dreamed up."

"You think these guys could be both lying about what's actually going on?" Ashley asked.

"Anyone could be lying but, actually, as weird as this whole thing is, I think they might both be telling the truth," Tim replied. "Then again, criminals *always* claim innocence…"

"These guys aren't doing that, though," said Ashley. "They've admitted their roles in it all."

"True, but they are both claiming they had no choice," Tim said. "At least, for now, we have this name - Rayna Cunningham," he said as he glanced at the name he'd recorded in his notepad. "Let's delve into the system and see if we can find anything out about her. If Manson was telling the truth, this Rayna has been undertaking some serious fraud. Might be something more about her that we find out if we look deep enough."

# CHAPTER 13

After searching for her name online and in various systems, Tim found nothing about Rayna Cunningham. It raised questions about whether the vet or the hacker had been telling the truth.

"Well, we knew there was always a chance that they both told a similar story as a way to put us off the real scent," Ashley said quietly when they considered there was nothing out there at all about the name they'd searched for. "But if this Rayna *is* responsible for skimming big money off a big corporation, how could she have avoided notice for so long? Surely something that size wouldn't be her first rip-off attempt..."

"Yeah, but remember that Liam said it didn't look like she'd been behind the coding of that particular fraudulent activity," said Tim. "He sounded pretty sure that all she'd done was be the person who inserted the code into her workstation computer to activate the process. Someone else is behind the program itself."

"Jesus," said Ashley as she breathed out deeply. "How many layers are there gonna be to this case?"

Tim smiled at her.

"Every layer we uncover is a layer closer to the truth," he said. Well used to seeing her grow frustrated when investigations seemed like they might never end, he found it refreshing to see her express her determination to solve the case.

"Well, I guess the good thing is that these attempts to hurt the Templetons by using a frigging *tiger* mean that it's far less likely to happen a third time," said Ashley. "Whoever is ultimately behind all of this, *must* be less likely to try it again, surely. Whoever it is, they must know that we're here investigating, and that the park must be increasing their security even more now that it's happened twice."

"True," said Tim. "It'd be good to know who was behind making it happen the first time. Both of these guys - Samson and Manson - have talked openly about having played their part in this last effort with the tiger. Neither have said they were a part of the first attempt."

"It's not a huge city," said Ashley.

"If the direction is being provided from a distance, whoever's behind this doesn't need to be in this city," Tim said. "They could be on the other side of the world, for all we know."

"If someone's going to that amount of effort to hurt the Templetons from the other side of the world, then they must have done something pretty big to piss someone off!" Ashley said, her mind pondering the possibility. "They're a lawyer and a surgeon. In what way could someone from far away have suffered enough to want to even try this weird plan?"

"I dunno, but I'm sending through a request to the guys at the office to see if they can track any correspondence, or some contact of any kind, to or from Greg Samson and Liam Manson around the date that this all happened," said Tim. "Both of them indicated that they'd received their instructions via phone, and they also received threats against their loved ones. That means they received them from someone, or at least somewhere. If we can find that out, it might help us out."

"Good idea," Ashley agreed.

# CHAPTER 14

"Off to see the Templetons again today then?" Tim asked Ashley as they sat in the hotel breakfast room the following morning.

"Yeah, I think we need to," said Ashley before taking a further sip of her coffee. "This Rayna might be a past client of Alana's, or a relative of a past client. We also don't yet know if the Templetons are somehow associated with Liam Manson. Even though he made it sound like he didn't know them, I want to run his name past them to make sure."

"Well, hopefully we'll get the phone and email records for both Manson and Samson soon," said Tim. "The guys said they'd have it all back to me by lunchtime today at the latest."

"Good," Ashley said, nodding. "In the meantime, where is your gut at as far as everything we've already heard goes? Anything leap out at you through your subconscious in the middle of the night?"

Tim grinned at her while he shook his head.

"Only one of us usually has subconscious clarity during sleep when we're on a case, Ash, and it isn't me!" he teased her. "But as far as my gut goes, yeah, I do believe what we've been told by everyone so far. I expect there's going to be a kink in at least one person's story, but for now, I think the players did what they've told us they did."

"And for the reason they gave? That their loved ones were threatened?" Ashley asked.

"It's feasible," said Tim. "But let's see if Alana recognizes these new names."

Half an hour later, as they pulled up to the Templeton residence, Ashley noted that both of their cars were in the driveway.

"We're in luck," she said. "Once again, they seem to both be at home."

"Now let's hope that they have some information that will prove useful to us in getting this case sorted and closed," said Tim. "They've both been surprisingly closed off till now."

Before they'd reached the front door, they saw it open.

"Oh, agents, I was just about to head into work," Steven said on seeing them. "I'm expected in the operating theatre in forty minutes."

"We only have a few questions, Mr. Templeton," Tim said. After a moment of what looked like uncertainty, Tim was glad to see Steven stand aside and welcome Ashley and Tim inside.

"Oh ... hello," Alana said, obviously surprised when the two agents entered the living room. "We ... we weren't expecting you. You'll have to excuse the mess."

Glancing around, Ashley had no idea what mess the woman was talking about, but ignored the comment.

"We just have a couple of names we'd like to run by you to see if you've heard of either of them," said Ashley as they all at down. "I know you haven't worked for a while, Mrs. Templeton, but if you could tell us if these people were either someone who you represented, or someone related or you've heard of in relation to who you've represented, that would be a great help."

"Of course," Alana said, nodding. "Who are they?"

"The first is Liam Manson," Tim said as he watched the faces of the Templetons carefully. "Is he a past client at all?"

"No," said Alana. "Manson … no, I don't recall ever having dealt with him either as a client or as someone associated with one. Sometimes, however, there are people associated with these clients but they wouldn't have talked about them to me."

"Yes, that is fine," said Tim. "The other name we have is Rayna Cunningham…"

As soon as he said that name, he saw Steven go almost white. Tim watched as Alana stepped in to answer the question. He was impressed by Steven's efforts to look neutral, even if the effort wasn't quite a success.

"No, I have never represented her either…" Alana said, believing the question was directed at her. When she glanced at Steven, after noticing how the agents were both looking at him, she saw a look on his face that she'd seen before. "What?" she asked, glancing around each of the three faces.

Steven, on hearing the name, told himself to remain absolutely still and not give anything away. When he saw Alana look at him with a question on her face, he felt a very familiar wave of guilt flow over him. He hadn't felt it in a while, but there had been a time when it had weighed on him heavily almost every day.

Alana watched as her husband abruptly stood up and walked a few feet away, as if going to leave the room. Instead of walking out completely, she saw him then stop and seem to take some time to regard his options.

"Steven?" she asked, calling out to him. "What is it? Do you *know* this person?"

Ashley watched the interaction, also eager to hear the answer to the question. Generally, it was Tim who could read people the best. At that moment, there was no deeper analysis needed to see that Steven Templeton was hiding something.

# CHAPTER 15

The silence was intense and long as three people seated in the living area looked at one another but kept returning their sight to the one standing. When Steven had stood silent and still for several minutes, Ashley watched Alana stand as if to approach him. There was no escaping the look of concern on her face.

"Steven, what's going on?" Alana asked. "I want to know! Do you *know* this person?"

Steven wanted to deny everything but he couldn't. He'd been dishonest in having the affair. That had meant lying to his wife two times a week, over an extended length of time. Although he'd changed since then, and regarded himself as a better man since he'd ended it, the consideration to lie was there. It had remained dormant for three years, but it was easily threatening to surface. To stop himself from being deceitful any more, he slowly turned around to face everyone.

"Yes," he said when he'd almost summoned the courage to be entirely truthful. "She's..." he started to say, silently hoping that the agents might guess without him having to say the words he'd dreaded having to for three long years. His silent plea wasn't acknowledged in any way. He turned to face Alana, preparing to possibly break the wall of solidarity they'd worked so hard to build again over recent years. "I'm so sorry, Alana..."

Tim and Ashley watched the uncomfortable scene begin to play out. Steven had told them that he'd had an affair, and he'd kept news of that from Alana. While Ashley wanted Steven to say straight out what had happened, she could see he was struggling. In the interest of getting to the bottom of what they needed to know for the investigation, she decided to edge things along.

"Rayna Cunningham, Mr. Templeton," Ashley said, commanding his attention. "She was the one?"

Tim glanced at his partner in surprise. He loved how direct Ashley could be, but she was usually a little bit more discreet in such situations - and subtle.

Steven looked at her, then at Alana, and back at Ashley before he spoke, his voice barely able to be heard.

"Yes," he finally answered, not wanting to go into any further detail until or unless he absolutely had to.

"The one ... what?" Alana asked, feeling an almost familiar dread flow over her. When her husband looked at her but said nothing, she took a step closer to him. "The one ...*what*?!"

"I ... I'm so sorry, Alana. I had an affair with her," Steven finally blurted out.

Alana felt the strength of her heart beating increase as she heard her husband's words. They were words that indicated a level of dishonesty she'd never expected to come from his mouth.

"How long?" she asked as tears appeared that she didn't try to stop. She'd never expected to hear her husband say the words that he was at that moment.

"Alana, please," Steven started to say as he felt his eyes also betray the horror he felt over what he'd done.

"*How long*?!" Alana screamed at him.

"It was years ago," said Steven.

"That doesn't answer my question," said Alana.

"Two years," Steven said, not daring to move from where he stood. "It lasted for two years."

Alana broke her gaze on him and turned away. Her husband had just admitted that he'd cheated on her for two years. She'd known things were rocky for a while, but hearing him say what he had…

"That was why you pulled away from me," she said, turning to look at him again. "Were you going to *leave* me for her?"

Steven was so surprised by the question that he had to formulate the answer in his head before he replied.

"Alana, I saw her for two years, and it was over with, three years ago," he said. "I ended it because I love you and I love our family…"

"*Love* our family?" Alana asked through her tears of what appeared to be weeping. "You can't say that you love your family when you're prepared to do that."

"That's not true," Steven said quietly. He suspected that the conversation with his wife would continue well into the future, but he was also aware that he was scheduled to do a surgery that was at the top end of the life-threatening spectrum. Hating to do so right at that moment, he turned away from his wife and faced the agents. "Rayna Cunningham is who I was seeing back then, but I haven't seen or heard from her for years. I can't believe that she'd … do *anything* like this!"

"Is there any chance that, after you broke off the affair, she was unstable?" Tim asked. "During your time with her, did you see *anything* about her that made you think she was unstable?"

"No!" said Steven. "If I'd seen anything like that, I wouldn't have seen her for as long as I did…"

"Sometimes, sex plays with people's heads, Mr. Templeton," Ashley said. "Could you have perhaps been looking at her through rose-colored glasses?"

Steven took a moment to consider the question. Could he have been regarding his past lover in a better light than he should have? It had been so long since he'd allowed himself to think about her, he had to concede that maybe he didn't know her - or at least correctly remember her - at all.

"I don't know," he finally admitted. "Maybe. I'd be surprised if she'd held onto anything about me for this long, but I don't know. I haven't heard from her so I don't know what her state of mind is like," he continued before looking at his wife. The extreme look of displeasure he saw was heartbreaking, but he couldn't shake the knowledge that someone else was in a life-threatening situation, and he was their surgeon. "I'm sorry, but I am expected in surgery. Can we … I know you're doing this investigation and it's important, but can we please continue this after the surgery I need to perform? I should be done in about five hours."

"It would be handy if you can give us an address or some form of contact for Ms. Cunningham," Tim said.

Steven looked horrified at the idea of handing over any contact details for his ex-lover.

"I deleted her mobile number from my phone, so I can't give you her number," he said, aware of time passing. "But I can write down her address - or at least, the address I used to see her at."

Tim glanced at Ashley and then nodded at Steven. After handing his notepad to Steven and watching him write down details, he accepted it back.

"Thank you," Steven said before moving toward Alana. When she replied with only the movement of turning her body so that her back was to him, he was regretful that he had to get to work, but he couldn't put someone's physical suffering ahead of the emotional suffering of him and his wife. "I … we can talk about this later, Alana."

After he walked out of the room, Ashley watched Mrs. Templeton return to her seat and place her head in her hands.

"We're so sorry that you found out about this like this," Ashley said quietly. It was a long while before she saw Alana raise her head and look directly at her.

"Did you *know* that my husband had an affair?" Alana asked. "You knew, and you didn't share that with me?"

"That…" Ashley started to reply. "We're trying to find out who tried to hurt you, Mrs. Templeton."

"Well, it seems like it wasn't just one person who's hurt me, doesn't it," Alana said, her voice thick with sarcasm and not sounding at all like the usual tone of composure they'd heard from her previously. "After all that, it took three of you to do that," she continued as she stood up and began to pace. "I think you'd better leave. I have nothing more to say to you."

Ashley and Tim quietly did as they'd been asked.

# CHAPTER 16

"I can't say that I feel very good about that," Tim said when they'd climbed into the car. "In fact, I feel like shit, to be completely honest."

"Yeah, I know what you mean, but it wasn't you or me who cheated," Ashley said. "Even if we hadn't been investigating this, that news could have come out at any time, and in any way."

"True," Tim agreed. "Still, what a way to find out that your husband's been shagging someone else."

"And that would not be our problem," said Ashley. "At least we have a connection now between the Templetons and the woman who seems to be behind all of this."

"Now we just have to find her," said Tim before starting to enter into his maps app the address that Steven had provided.

"Address that he gave you legit?" Ashley asked, half expecting it might not be.

"The address is legit," Tim said, nodding. "Now we just have to work out if she does still live there."

"And if he's telling the truth," said Ashley.

"What is it about his story that you doubt?" Tim asked, curious. "Surely he wouldn't make up having an affair, or try and deny it was with her after we said her name."

"I don't believe anything till it's proven, Timmy Boy," Ashley replied grinning at him. "You know that!"

"It does seem like everyone we've spoken to have all given us information remarkably freely and easily," Tim said. "Only one way to know for sure, though."

"Yep," Ashley said as she pushed her foot to the floor a bit more. "Let's go see what this woman has to say."

"Just out of curiosity, what exactly can this woman be charged with even if we do find her?" Tim asked as he pondered the whole situation. "Attempted murder seems a stretch."

Ashley took some time to internally ask the question before she could provide some insight into her views.

"Well, murder - or attempted murder - has to be based on intent, doesn't it," she said. "I'm guessing that's what would need to be proved - that she came up with this elaborate plan to use a tiger to murder the wife of her ex-lover."

"Yeah, but even if we find her, we can't arrest her for that today," Tim said. "We've got hearsay but not enough evidence."

"True," Ashley agreed. "If it's proven, the one thing she has done - and left a trail for the Bureau tech guys to find - is insert that code into the power provider's system and steal money from them and their customers."

Tim nodded but felt doubt.

"Still only hearsay," he said. "We've only heard that from Manson. We need…" he said as he pulled out his phone. "We need the guys back at HQ to prove if that is right."

Ashley nodded in agreement. For the most part, proving what had happened was something that happened fairly long after she and Tim had completed any investigation. While she hoped that all that they'd learned would prove to be not only true, but also a basis for the conspirator to be charged, she knew that nothing was ever guaranteed in getting the bad guys of the world charged and put away.

She quietly listened to the call that Tim made, explaining what he wanted the computer forensics team to delve into. In hindsight, they could have requested that to be done much earlier. Hindsight. What a wonderful thing.

"They'll let us know for sure that Manson's been telling us the truth about what he was doing, and what he found out about Rayna Cunningham in the process," Tim said.

"Good. For now, we can at least talk to her and hear what she has to say," said Ashley.

"Fingers crossed that we can find her to do that," Tim said, beginning to develop a strong feeling of uncertainty.

# CHAPTER 17

Pulling up to the address that had been provided to the agents by Steven Templeton, both were surprised.

"Not quite the palace I'd kind of expected someone who's been skimming money of that magnitude to live in, I have to say," Ashley said as she turned off the engine.

"Best way to hide wealth gained illegally is to not show it off," Tim said.

"True," said Ashley as they began to prepare to approach the home. "Well, let's go and see what this woman has to say. If nothing else, it'll be interesting to see who a man like Steven Templeton would almost give up his wife and kids for."

As they walked up the path to the front door of the home, Ashley and Tim both took notice of the state of the front yard. If Rayna Cunningham was purposely intent on making it seem like she was poor rather than rich, she was doing a pretty good job of it. There was nothing about the property that made it look like she had any money to spare at all.

"If you're looking for her, she's at work," they heard someone call out before they reached the home's front door.

Backing up from the point they'd reached, Ashley and Tim saw an elderly man watching them from across the fence to one side.

"Thank you," Ashley said as she walked over to

him. "We're looking for a Ms. Cunningham. Can you confirm this is her home, Mr. …?"

"Thompson," the man said. "Bob Thompson. And yes, that's Rayna's home." He paused a moment, looking over both agents from head to toe. "She in trouble?"

"We just have some questions for her," Tim said. "Do you know her well?"

"Of course," Bob said, nodding. "Been neighbors for around ten years, if not more."

"What can you tell us about her?" Tim asked and saw Bob shrug his shoulders.

"Nice enough lass," he said. "I've never seen her in any kind of trouble since I've known her. Seems to keep to herself, working hard and living a quiet life."

"No husband?" asked Ashley. "Partner?"

"Not that I've ever seen," said Bob. "There was a gentleman visiting for a while - someone rich, he looked like - but I haven't seen him for a few months now."

"A few *months*?" Ashley asked, the timeline striking her curiosity. "Would you happen to know the name of this man?"

"No, I was never introduced to him properly, even though he said hello a couple of times when I was out here and he was coming or going," Bob said.

"Do you have any idea what he did for a living?" Tim asked.

"No, although he did say one time that he was in a hurry to get to the hospital," Bob replied. "Don't know if that meant he worked there or not."

Tim and Ashley exchanged a glance.

"Is there anything else you can tell us either

about the man, or about Rayna?" Ashley asked. "Anything you can think of about what kind of people either of them is would be wonderful."

"No, there's nothing I can think of," Bob said. "That is to say, Rayna's a nice enough woman. Seems to like to keep to herself, but she works hard and supports herself well. Works weekends a lot, even though she's said she only *needs* to work during the week. Not sure why she does the weekend stuff. Mentioned once that they don't pay her hardly anything for the extra hours. That's crazy, if you ask me. Why would you work extra hours in any job if you didn't need to and you weren't getting paid decent enough for it?"

"Yes, that is curious," Tim said. "Alright, well, thank you, Bob. You've been a great help…"

"Do you know where she works?" Bob called out before the agents hopped in the car. "The power place - you know it?"

"Yes," Tim called back. "Thank you."

In the car, Ashley's mind was busy. They'd assumed that Rayna would be home because it was the weekend. It hadn't occurred to either agent that Rayna would be at work outside of standard office hours.

"Is the electricity corporation office open today?" she asked Tim and saw his face reflect the same level of thought that she knew hers would.

"I wouldn't have thought so," Tim replied. "But it sounds like it must be. I thought that, since she's an admin worker, she'd be working normal nine-to-five, Monday to Friday hours."

"And she does, from what the neighbor just indicated," said Ashley. "Works regular office hours, but *chooses* to go in on the weekends as well."

"Maybe that's got something to do with all this money skimming," Tim suggested. "Does she siphon the money while she's in the office on weekends or something?"

"Seems a bit extreme to do that when everything can be done through the Internet," said Ashley. "Although, I guess it might make it easier to do something direct and in the office? I dunno. I'm not a computer nerd so have no idea how it could all work if she is taking all that money."

"Head over to their head office then, and see if we can see her?" Tim asked and saw Ashley smile.

"Yeah, but let's get you fed first," she teased. "Lunch?"

"Why Special Agent Ashley Power, I thought you'd never ask," Tim replied, grinning.

# CHAPTER 18

Settled into a booth in a quiet restaurant in the center of town, Ashley and Tim took their time perusing the menu. Although they each had an incredibly healthy appetite, both agents were bothered by things that they'd just learned.

"Are you two ready to order?" they heard a waitress ask, encouraging them to look up from the menus they'd been blankly staring at.

"Umm," Tim said as he forced himself to focus on the card he held. "I'll have the chicken and fries, thanks."

"Yes, same for me, thanks," said Ashley, resulting in a particular kind of glance from her partner. "What?" she asked Tim as the waitress left their table.

"You hardly ever go for deep fried," Tim said, smiling at her. "Something must have you rattled. Come on. Out with it. Share with me what you're thinking."

"I was just thinking about how Bob Thompson said that Rayna Cunningham has had some guy at her home as recently as three months ago," Ashley said. "Some guy that was regularly going to the *hospital*."

"Yeah, I automatically thought about Steven Templeton when the neighbor said that too," said Tim. "Doesn't mean it's him, though. The hospital must have hundreds of staff in it. Who's to say if she didn't begin dating another guy from there?"

"True," Ashley replied, nodding. "It's not at all impossible. It just seems like such a big coincidence - a little *too* big, maybe?"

"Well, if it is Steven Templeton, he's lied," Tim said in contemplation. "And if he's lied about that…"

"What else has he lied about?" Ashley pondered.

"Is that all that's on your mind?" Tim asked. "That Steven Templeton might not have ended his affair three years ago after all?"

"No," said Ashley. "The other aspect is the style of living of Rayna. If she's been siphoning off all that money, what's she doing with it?"

"We only saw the front yard and exterior of her house," said Tim. "For all we know, it could be decked out like a palace on the inside."

"Hmm," mumbled Ashley. "I don't know what to make of this Rayna woman, given what we've heard about her from the different angles."

"Well," Tim said as their meals were placed in front of them. "I'm guessing you'll be able to figure her out soon enough. We know where she is today…"

"We know where her neighbor *thinks* she is today," Ashley quickly rectified.

"Right. We know where she *possibly could be* today," Tim said, partially in teasing. "We'll track her down, and when we do, we should be able to formulate a much clearer picture of this woman."

"And hopefully gain some understanding about why she's done all this," Ashley added before taking a bite of her meal. "Yum, this chicken is real good. Great choice, partner!"

# CHAPTER 19

Walking around the exterior of the large headquarters of the local electricity provider, Tim and Ashley tried to find a way in. Although they'd been told that Rayna would be working inside the building, there was no sign of life that they could see from the outside. The main doors were locked and there was no security guard or anyone else to be seen.

"There's not going to be any getting into there right now, Ash," Tim said when they'd checked there were no additional entry points around the building. "We could get a number for Rayna, but then she'd know we're looking for her."

"If she's in there, she's going to have to come out," said Ashley, glancing around. "Two other cars in the carpark. Let's run their plates and see if one happens to come back as hers."

"On it," Tim said as he began walking back to the car.

Settled into the car, he quickly put through a request for details of the owners of both cars that were nearby.

"Should only take a few minutes," he said, turning to face Ashley. "And if we get confirmation that she is here? That's not a place to try and force an entry into, I'm thinking."

"If she's in there, she has to come out sometime," Ashley said. "She won't know we're looking for her, unless her neighbor's contacted her."

"Or Steven Templeton," Tim said and saw Ashley nod.

"Good point," she said. "If he's lied about his affair with her being over, he could very well be talking to her on the phone right now, telling her that we're probably looking for her."

"Yeah, but what I don't get is if he *is* having an affair with this woman, why would he have told us about it at all?" Tim asked. "I mean, even before that uncomfortable scenario at the house last time we were there, when he admitted to his wife that he'd cheated, he'd already told us about having seen someone else. He didn't need to do that. Chances are that we might not have found out about it at all, even after we learned her name from the vet and the hacker."

"True," Ashley agreed. "Maybe he's done it all just to throw us off the track of something he's actually involved in. The affair could be real, but it also could be some kind of ruse, especially if she's the one who coordinated the men to take the tiger in the first place."

"Husband tries to have his wife killed?" Tim asked. "A fairly common scenario that we've seen far too many times. It's a bit extreme to use the tiger as the way to do it, and bold trying it not once but twice, but I guess it's definitely a possibility."

Before Ashley could reply with her perspective, Tim's phone sounded.

"Number plates confirmed," Tim said when he hung up the call. "That blue one is hers," he continued, pointing to a small blue hatchback parked between them and the building entrance.

"Hmm. Well, I guess that gives us the answer

about whether she is actually inside the building right now or not," said Ashley, pondering options as she looked at her watch. "Problem is, we don't know what time she'll finish. If she's in there, but not for actual work, she could leave in five minutes or in five hours."

"Stakeout time," Tim said, grinning at her.

Ashley chuckled quietly. As far as partners went, he was the best she'd ever had. He was brilliant at his job, but he was also the easiest to get on with when they were in the quiet times of a case or when they were under pressure.

"Guess so," she said. "Better get comfortable then!"

Although Tim continued to grin at her, his mind was active. He had his work laptop with him, and a full and diverse range of professionals back at headquarters, ready to delve into whatever they needed to find out. He just needed to figure out what exactly he and Ashley still needed to know about each of the people they'd learned of so far.

Someone attempting to commit murder wasn't a situation they'd never dealt with in their careers, and some criminals had some pretty wacky motives and methods to their madness. To even consider using an animal for such a job had to take a particular kind of mind, to say the least.

"You're thinking rather hard," Ashley teased him as she watched his face. "What's going on in that head of yours, Moore?"

"I was just trying to piece together all that we've learned so far, and what we still need to find out," Tim said. "On the surface, everything seems pretty straightforward…"

"Except for a tiger being used as a weapon,"

Ashley said, chuckling.

"Apart from that," said Tim, nodding. "But you used the key word that I was just thinking about - weapon. Yeah, of course it's a weird way to hurt someone, but the tiger *was* just a weapon. Someone could have just as easily used a gun or a knife, or any other horrifying way that we know people are killed."

"True," Ashley agreed. "Still a bit of an odd choice for a weapon."

"Yeah, as far as weapons go, even removing the weird aspect of it, it's not a very effective one to use," Tim continued. "I mean, yes, if the tiger had been able to attack Alana or her son, it could have been devastating, but there would never be a guarantee that a tiger *would* attack them. That particular tiger has grown up around humans, and while the vet said that it was a wild animal at heart, it still seems a bit of a gamble to use it as a way to hurt or kill anyone."

"I agree," said Ashley. "Whatever reason Rayna had for wanting to do this - and I think it's fair to assume that she might have done it to somehow get Steven's wife out of the way so Rayna could have him all to herself - why would she choose that particular path to do it?"

"And was it her who even wanted this to happen?" Tim asked. When he saw Ashley consider the question, he considered it further himself. "It looks like there's a chance that Steven Templeton has been lying about the affair having been over with for years. What if this isn't about Rayna wanting him all to herself, and trying to get rid of Alana to facilitate that? What if..."

"Steven did it," Ashley suggested as she

pondered the possibility. "Steven wanted his wife gone so that he could be with Rayna, and together they came up with this plan. That could explain why Rayna looks like the one responsible for all of this, but it was a *man* who called Greg and Liam to give instructions about that night."

"It also explains why both instances with the tiger occurred when Steven was away at the golf charity event," said Tim.

"It's a way for him to have an alibi," Ashley said and saw Tim nod.

"Exactly. It's still only a hypothesis, though. The only aspect of this that seems certain *is* that Rayna facilitated everything," he said. "What we don't know is whether she did it all for her - to fight to have him all to herself - or she did it all for *him*."

"The other aspect, that you know could be a possibility, is that she could be the scapegoat for Steven," said Ashley. "Have we looked into whether there's been any life insurance policies taken out on Alana this past year?"

"Good thinking," Tim said as he sent a message through to the support team. "What doesn't sit well with me is that it's still dangerous, yes, but also unknown, what using a wild animal would result in. That day that the tiger went to the home, Steven would have known that he and his older kids would be out at the time, but his youngest son was at home. Even if Alana did manage to keep herself and her son safe that day, it would be a huge gamble to assume that the tiger wouldn't kill that kid. Does Steven seem like the kind of guy who might want to be rid of his kids?"

"Those that do, don't always look the part of parents who want their kids gone," said Ashley as she felt emotional at the thought. She'd long been considering where she might be able to fit having a child into her life. The sadness she got to experience through cases involving children sometimes made her question if she wanted to bring a child into the world or not. It could be a happy world for children. It could just as easily be a nightmare.

Tim watched her face as they delved into the subject of kids. He knew her feelings about wanting to be a mom one day. Personally, he thought she'd make a great mother. He'd told her that whenever they'd talked about the options for her. Despite how much he knew she wanted to have children, he also knew that she felt the same dilemma that many women faced - they wanted to be full-time moms, but they also wanted to be in full-time employment. With Ashley, Tim also knew that part of the difficulty was that she wanted to also put her job ahead of prioritizing being in a relationship. On that note, he could have happily made her an offer that could provide her with the life that she wanted. He never had. That was knowledge that he'd long ago decided was best kept to himself.

"Is that her?" he heard Ashley ask, rousing him from his thoughts, and the emotions that had threatened to show.

When Tim turned and followed her line of sight, he saw a woman moving towards the car they'd identified as Rayna's. As soon as she was within a couple of yards of it, both agents got out of their car to approach her.

"Rayna Cunningham!" Ashley called out and saw the woman turn and look at them. It was a kind of moment when Tim and Ashley had both seen criminals turn and flee rather than talk to investigators. Ashley was relieved to see that Rayna Cunningham had no such desire.

"Yes?" she asked when the agents approached her.

"Are you Rayna Cunningham?" asked Tim. Seeing her nod, he, too, was glad that she looked so relaxed and not at all inclined to do a runner. "I'm Special Agent Moore and this is Special Agent Power. We'd like to ask you some questions."

"About what?" Rayna asked as she glanced from one agent to the other.

"Firstly, about your involvement with a tiger being let loose on a family home recently," Tim said and monitored her face for her reaction.

"I don't know what you're talking about," Rayna said, turning away to unlock her car.

"Are you sure about that?" Ashley asked.

Both agents watched as Rayna stopped in her progress of opening her car door, and instead turned to face them again.

"Yes, I know about it," she said quietly. "I … I know the family."

"All of them?" asked Tim. "Or just one in particular?"

"Steven Templeton … he's someone that … he's someone that I used to see," Rayna said as her face grew red.

"Used to?" Tim asked for clarification.

"Yes," Rayna answered, nodding. "It's been over for a long time now."

"How long?" asked Ashley.

Rayna shrugged her shoulders and glanced from one agent to the other again.

"I dunno," she said. "Maybe two or three years or so?"

"Not three months ago?" asked Tim.

"No," Rayna replied, shaking her head. "I knew Steven years ago. It wasn't my finest hour, I can tell you, sleeping with a married man, but I met him and, well, I fell in love with him. For a while, he talked about leaving his wife, so he could be with me full-time. Just words, they were. I don't think he ever intended to leave her."

"So you took matters into your own hands..." Tim suggested but was surprised to see the woman in front of him look so confused.

"I'm sorry," she said. "I don't understand. Has something happened to Steven?"

"No, we are referring to the tiger that was delivered to their home, presumably to cause harm," Ashley said.

"I still don't understand," Rayna said again. "When I read about that happening, I thought it had just escaped from the park up the road, and curiosity had driven it to walk onto that property. That's what the newspaper article reported. Are you saying that someone *put* it there?"

"That is what we believe, yes," Ashley replied.

"But what has this got to do with me?" Rayna asked. "I gather that you're talking to me because you know that I was involved with Steven in the past," she said. "But what has our time together back then have to do with this?"

"You work here?" Tim asked, nodding towards the large head office of the electricity corporation.

"Yes," said Rayna.

"We understand that you work in the administration department," Tim said and saw her nod. "It has been brought to our attention that you have been stealing money from your employer."

The look of horror on Rayna's face was a surprise to Tim and Ashley. Although they were well used to some of the most intense criminals being able to look completely innocent, everything about their interaction with Rayna Cunningham looked authentic, including her surprise.

"I would *never*!" Rayna exclaimed. "How … why would you think that?"

"Do you know a gentleman by the name of Greg Samson?" Ashley asked.

"No. Who is he?" Rayna asked.

"What about Liam Manson?" asked Tim, his curiosity growing. The more questions they asked of the woman in front of them, the more she looked like she didn't know anything at all about whatever they were asking. Not that the look of innocence ever guaranteed that someone being questioned *was* innocent.

"No, I've never heard of either of them," Rayna replied. "I'm sorry, but I really am confused. What's this actually about? What do these two people have to do with my having known Steven in the past?"

Ashley remained quiet for a long while, watching the woman and quietly wondering if someone had perhaps gotten their wires crossed - or if they were in the company of a sociopath.

"How are things between you and Steven now?" she finally asked after considering a variety of options.

"Now? There's nothing between us *now*!" Rayna said, sounding like she had to try hard to keep calm. "Look, I met Steven Templeton *years* ago. We had a mutual friendship of sorts - and yes, by that I mean that we were lovers. We met years ago, we saw each other for a couple of years, and then he ended it."

"What reason did he give for ending it?" Tim asked.

"He didn't - not really," Rayna replied. "One minute, he was coming over to my place a lot, and talking about leaving his wife to come be with me full-time. Next minute, he was saying that he didn't want to do it anymore. I didn't ask why. He didn't want to see me, and that was quite enough for me to deal with. I really didn't need to know anything else about his decision - or particularly want to."

"Were you upset by it?" Ashley asked.

"Damn right I was! I gave two years of my life to that man! And he was the one who kept talking about leaving his wife. *I* didn't bring that subject up - *he* did! Why would a guy do that and then not follow through with it? Fucked me off no end, I can tell you!"

"Hope you don't mind me saying, but you look as if you're *still* pissed off by it," Tim said.

"I..." Rayna started to say before presenting more of a look of defeat. "Look, I got involved with a married man who I ... yeah, I probably did fall in love with. I wish I hadn't. It's something that I regret to this day, but it happened. Was I happy when he broke things off? No, of course I wasn't happy. I'd been seeing him for a long time, and we had established what I thought was a really strong rapport. It did hurt. But am I still thinking about it? No - not till this happened anyway."

"This...?" Tim asked for clarification.

"This tiger thing - the tiger going to their house," said Rayna. "I wouldn't have even noticed that if it had only been the house that was shown in the article, but it had a photo of the family so I was reminded of Steven again."

"You didn't know it was their house?" asked Ashley.

"No, of course not. I never went to their home," Rayna replied. "Steven used to come to my place whenever he wanted to see me. I didn't even know where he lived. I never *wanted* to know. I knew that he had a whole other life that I wasn't a part of. I didn't need to see it."

"Hmm," Tim muttered, thinking. "Back to your job… do you deny stealing money from your employer?"

"Yes! How would I even do that?" Rayna asked. "I don't have anything to do with payments! I'm not on the front counter, taking cash from people. I'm out the back, working all day in a dinky little office where I do basic processing of some external accounts. I don't have access to any money in there," she said, pointing at the building. "Why would you think that I'd have done something like that, anyway?"

"Has anyone in recent times given you a USB stick to use in your work computer?" asked Tim, disregarding the question she'd asked.

"No…" Rayna said, shaking her head. "Should they have? I'm sorry, but I'm so confused. What exactly is going on?"

"You're sure?" Ashley asked, also choosing to ignore a question Rayna had presented to the agents. "Nobody gave you a USB stick, or sent you one…"

"No," Rayna said again. "And even if someone had tried that, it wouldn't have worked in there," she said, pointing at her workplace once more. "The terminals are closed off to anything like that. I once tried to take a pen drive in just so that I could use the office printer to print off a copy of a bank statement. Couldn't access the drive at all. When I asked someone about it, they said that nobody except upper management have the authority on their terminals to access any external media or drives like that."

As Tim ran through all that they'd learned on the case so far in his mind, he felt wary. Either Rayna was a very good liar, or other people they'd interacted with up till that moment had been the liars. At that moment, as he stood in front of her and heard her speak, it was difficult to determine which was right.

"Look, am I in trouble or something?" Rayna asked, her voice betraying how weary and concerned she felt. "You still haven't told me what's going on here, even though you appear to have gone out of your way to find me. Are you charging me with something?"

"No," said Tim. "But can I ask, are you seeing someone at the moment?"

"Not that it's any of your business, but no," Rayna replied.

"Have you been seeing anyone this past year?" Tim pushed.

"Yes," Rayna answered after a lengthy sigh of what sounded like growing annoyance. "Earlier this year, I was seeing a man. What does this have to do with anything?"

"What was his name?" asked Ashley. "Please, Rayna. This may help us to find out why your name has been dragged into our investigation," she added as a way to placate the woman that she could see was beginning to grow more than a little impatient.

"Andrew," Rayna said. "But don't ask me for his last name. We were seeing each other for a few months, purely for fun. I didn't give him my last name, and I didn't ask for his."

"And when did this end? When did you last see him?" Tim asked.

"Last saw him about … maybe three or four months ago," Rayna said. "Said he had to head back to whatever southern town he was up here from. I didn't ask any questions. It was what it was, I had some fun with him, and I was happy to know as little about him as possible."

"Alright. I think we have all that we need for now," Ashley said, looking at Tim and seeing him nod. "We will be wanting to speak to you again, however. Is there a number we can call you on?"

"Sure," Rayna said before reading her number out and then turning to open her car door.

"Oh, one more thing. Do you work normal office hours here?" asked Tim.

"Normally," Rayna replied as she nodded. "Right now, my father needs some extra help financially, so I've taken on some weekend work here as a cleaner. It's not glamorous, but it helps me to keep him and me both set up. Is there anything else?"

"No, thank you," said Ashley. "We'll be in touch."

Taking only a step or two backward, Ashley and Tim watched her car leave the carpark before they turned to face one another.

"We have a lot that doesn't add up, Timmy Boy," Ashley said.

"Yeah, but now we do know one thing for sure," he said and saw her look at him with the expectation of clarification. "At least one person so far has been lying to us - and maybe, more than one of them."

Tim's phone ringing interrupted their chain of thought and conversation. When he'd hung up the call, Ashley saw a new level of seriousness on his face.

"What is it?" she asked, curious.

"Life insurance," said Tim. "A new policy was taken out on Alana Templeton seven months ago."

"That usually means only one thing when there's been a murder attempt. We need to go back to the start and refresh our findings so far," said Ashley. "Come on. Let's go buy some real good coffee, and take it back to the hotel. Either we've missed something, we haven't delved deep enough yet, or Alana Templeton's life insurance could be the ticket to the answers we need to find."

"It certainly presents us with more questions about her husband," Tim agreed.

# CHAPTER 20

As Ashley sat quietly, repeatedly running their conversation with Rayna Cunningham through her mind, she felt perplexed. Everything about their investigation had felt like it was moving forward in a straightforward manner. Everyone they'd spoken to had seemed genuine in their answers to the questions they'd been asked. When investigations flowed so easily, she did know that it was likely that something wasn't as it seemed. Knowing that didn't help her to feel any better at that moment.

"Have we been asking the right questions?" she asked Tim. When she saw him focus on her, she continued to speak as her self-doubt began to rear its head. "So far, everyone has answered our questions. Nobody's done a runner, like we're used to happening. Nobody's said they aren't going to talk, and then gone and gotten a lawyer. Nobody has done anything that makes them look, in any way, suspicious!"

Tim smiled sadly at her. He knew that tone. Most of the time, Ashley was one of the most confident people he'd ever met. Every now and then, however, she showed a side that was far less confident, and far more doubtful about her skills as an agent with the Bureau.

"That's exactly why we do this job, Ash," he said. "To solve cases, yes, but more than that, we're here to figure out who is behind these events, who is lying, and why. Let's just go over all of this again."

"Yeah, I know you're right," Ashley said in an effort to shift her thought pattern.

"Just as I always am, Special Agent Power," Tim teased her in an effort to make her smile. He was pleased when she did.

"As if," Ashley replied as she grinned at him. "Okay," she continued as she sat up straighter and reverted back into the role of a confident agent. "Let's go over everything and try…"

"Do," said Tim, cutting her sentence short. When he saw Ashley frown at him, he grinned again. "There is no try. There is only do, or do not."

"You learn that from a little green guy?" Ashley asked, rolling her eyes. "Anyway!"

"Anyway," Tim said, chuckling. "Okay, we know that Steven Templeton had an affair. I think the odds of him having lied about that are pretty slim, especially since he admitted the affair in front of his wife. That opens up the real possibility that his lover, Rayna, is behind all of this, trying to either take revenge on him for breaking up with her, or just wanting to be rid of his wife so that there's no longer any reason why Steven won't be able to be with her."

"Right!" said Ashley as she stood up and began to pace. "But both of them said their affair ended at least a couple of years ago, even though she appears to have been seeing someone from the hospital far more recently. Rayna also said that Steven never gave her any reason why he wanted to stop seeing her, whereas he told us that he did tell her that he wanted to focus on his marriage. He's also now happily settled with his wife…"

"Apparently," Tim said.

"Apparently," Ashley agreed, nodding. "Plus, like you say, we know that Rayna's been involved with at least one man since the affair ended."

"Yes, but that's only if the affair did end," said Tim. "If everything is as Rayna just told us, she hasn't seen Steven, and she has spent time with a guy named Andrew," Tim said. "If she was being honest, and this guy does actually exist, we don't know anything about him. Could he have something to do with this as well?"

"Maybe, although the timeline doesn't quite suit," said Ashley. "She said she was seeing him only till three months ago."

"Right, and she also stated that she was only seeing him for a few months," Tim said. "That means he *was* around when the first instance of Tigger getting out happened."

"Yeah, but not the second," said Ashley. "We have to explore all possibilities, though. Maybe he was one of the people who took part in getting Tigger to the Templeton home that first time around. He could have helped her with that, and have since left town to avoid any possibility of being associated with it."

"Someone to talk to and add to the list of possible suspects then?" Tim asked.

"Yeah, maybe," Ashley replied. "Rayna said she didn't know his last name."

"Doesn't always work, but we could try searching for his number," Tim suggested. "Get the guys to look through her call history? Maybe they can locate him that way as well."

"Yeah," Ashley said. "Hopefully, they'll find something that can help us eliminate him from having anything to do with this."

"It's always a long shot finding someone," said Tim.

"Especially if he's out of town now, like Rayna indicated…" Ashley started to say before she heard Tim's phone notification sound.

"Seems we don't have to search any more," Tim said minutes later, more than a little curious about the information he'd just opened in his email. "Wow, I think that was the fastest search I've ever seen."

"And? What's the result? Who is this *Andrew*?" Ashley asked, reading the confusion on his face when he'd been silent for a couple of minutes.

"In amongst Rayna's calls for three to six months ago, there's a number that repeats a lot … and belongs to someone we've already met," said Tim, looking at her. "Wayne Medici."

"Wayne Medici?" Ashley asked. "Tiger keeper?" she further asked and saw Tim nod. "Wayne Medici, the tiger keeper, is…"

"Someone that Rayna knows?" Tim asked as he considered the possibility. "That's definitely what this call log seems to indicate."

"Okay, but just how many calls were made between them over that time?" Ashley asked. "Could it be just a passing interaction?"

"Ahh, no," Tim said, glancing over the extensive list of phone calls again. "They messaged and called each other a *lot* over that time. With the stretch of time that I'm looking at, when their communication was active, I'm guessing that either he's the guy she's called Andrew, or they've been talking about how to do this crime."

"Tiger keeper and Steven Templeton's ex-lover,"

Ashley pondered. "An interesting but sound grouping for making this all happen."

"You think Rayna's lied about her involvement in all of this then?" Tim asked.

"If she's been liaising with him as much as you're saying, then yeah, maybe," said Ashley. "If she is still at the top of our suspect list, I don't want to bring too much attention to us looking into her movements and calls."

"Well, Rayna's neighbor said he saw the guy that she was seeing," said Tim. "He also said that the guy worked at the hospital, which still produces the possibility that it was Steven Templeton. That would align with the new life insurance policy that was taken out on Alana not too long ago."

"Yeah, true. We certainly can't ignore the life insurance. That's one of the most consistent motives for murder that we've seen in our job," Ashley agreed. "But going back to the neighbor … let's go and see him again, this time with photos of each of the main players in this event. Maybe he'll be able to pick out the guy that was visiting Rayna."

"That won't tell us what their relationship is to one another," Tim said.

"No, but at this stage, that may not matter," said Ashley. "We know that she was seeing Steven Templeton, but we have doubt about whether that was over with years ago. Instead, it's entirely feasible that they've actually continued to see each other, and are lying about it. There's also some connection here between Wayne Medici and Rayna Cunningham and, together, the two of *them* might have something to do with this."

"Alright, but I do think it'd be best if we go to speak to the next door neighbor when Rayna isn't home," Tim suggested.

"I agree," said Ashley. "Let's hold off on that till tomorrow when we know she'll be at work again..."

"And since it'll be a weekday, she should be away for the whole day, so there'll be no chance of her seeing us talking to Bob Thompson," Tim suggested. "Not that we could stop him telling her that we've been back to show him photos and ask questions, of course."

"Yep, that makes sense," Ashley said. "He probably is loyal to her, having known her for so many years, but you never know - if he suspects she's done something wrong, he could be just the right kind of law-abiding citizen who would dob in a neighbor if he thought they were doing something wrong. In the meantime, we need to look a little harder into who exactly Wayne Medici is."

# CHAPTER 21

Next day, Ashley and Tim assembled the photos they had of each of the men that they'd interviewed. During the night, they'd each received more information about the background of the tiger keeper, Wayne Medici. After reading through it all, both agreed that there was nothing about his background that implied he was capable of murder. In his background, they found no indication of him having broken the law at all.

"Okay, well, that hasn't proved too useful, but criminals are never seen as criminals until the day they get caught. Just because we haven't found anything out about him that makes him look suspicious, doesn't mean he isn't. Let's see what the neighbor tells us today," Tim said as they packed up and got ready to leave the hotel. "For all we know, it could have been Steven Templeton who was visiting Rayna after all."

"Do you *want* it to be him?" Ashley asked him, curious about how persistent he was being in wanting to roll with Steven Templeton as the suspect.

"I don't want it to be anyone in particular," Tim said, biting perfectly to her teasing. "But you know as well as I do that, when it comes to murder, most of the time it is the spouse or partner."

"Yeah, I know," Ashley replied, smiling at him. "Let's see where this path of questioning takes us.

So far, everyone who could be a suspect has been good at covering themselves as far as where and how they could have done it, or why."

"True, but this present puzzle, we can hopefully lock in as a fact," Tim said. "Let's go and see what Mr. Thompson has to tell us."

# CHAPTER 22

Pulling up to the street where Rayna Cunningham and Bob Thompson lived, Ashley and Tim took their time to look and make sure that Rayna had already left. The lack of a car in her driveway assured them that they might get to speak to her neighbor without her immediately knowing.

"If they're as close as he indicated last time we spoke to him, he probably is going to tell her about our visit anyway," Tim said as they made their way up the path to Bob Thompson's house.

"I know," said Ashley. "But at least we might get a head start in chasing up whoever the mystery man is that she was seeing."

"Not convinced it's Medici?" Tim asked her in surprise. "We've seen the phone records…"

Before Ashley could provide her opinion, the door in front of them opened.

"Agents," Mr. Thompson said. "Are you here to see me?"

"We are indeed, Mr. Thompson," Ashley replied. "We're hoping that you might be able to help us with something rather pressing."

"Oh, yes! Of course," Bob said as he stood back and opened his door wider. "Please come in."

"Thank you," said Ashley as she and Tim followed the elderly gentleman inside.

"Please sit down and tell me how I can be of assistance to you," Bob said as he sat in what looked, to Ashley, must have been his favorite chair for more than just a few years.

"When we spoke with you last time we were here, you mentioned a man that you'd seen coming and going from Rayna's house," Tim said.

"Yes, seemed a nice enough man," said Bob. "Didn't hesitate to say hello and tell me he was going to work. Works at the hospital, he said."

"Yes," Ashley said. "I wonder if you might be able to look through a few photographs, and tell us if the man you saw coming and going next door is among them?"

"Oh, yes," Bob said. "Just let me get my glasses."

When he'd readied himself and sat down again, Ashley passed the small selection of photos to him. After what looked like a few passes through the photos, she saw him select one and hold it up for her and Tim to see.

"This one," said Bob. "This is the man that I've seen coming and going - the one who works at the hospital. Haven't seen him for a couple of months now, however."

"But you're sure that he *is* the one that you saw and spoke to?" Tim asked.

"Oh, yes," Bob replied. "I have no doubt about that."

"And you haven't seen any of these others in the neighborhood at all?" Tim asked, prompting Bob to flick through the stack again.

"This man, perhaps?" Bob suggested, pulling a second photo from the pile.

Both agents watched as the elderly man studied the photo for a decent amount of time.

"Hmm," he finally said. "He does look familiar,

although not from recently. I think he might have been coming here before - a very long time ago - but I haven't seen him in recent months."

"Alright, well, thank you, Mr. Thompson," Ashley said. "We greatly appreciate you being able to do this for us."

"Is Rayna in some kind of danger from this man?" Bob asked. "She is a good woman, you know. Always been good to me, helping me with whatever I've had to ask for help with. I wouldn't like to see her get hurt."

"We aren't yet sure if she is in danger or not," Tim replied. "For the moment, we have a lot of questions to ask a lot of people, however we don't think there is any reason to mention this to Rayna and cause her any unnecessary alarm."

"Very well. I understand," said Bob as he stood to show the agents out. "I shan't mention it to her then. If you need anything more from me, you know where I am."

After Ashley and Tim said their goodbyes and walked to the car, both felt relieved that at least one part of the puzzle had fallen into place.

"Seems to be no doubt about it then," Ashley said, turning to face him as they each put on their seatbelt.

"Wayne Medici," said Tim. "He's in on this, and he's in on it with Rayna."

"Best we pay our local tiger keeper another visit."

# CHAPTER 23

Approaching the front gate of the wildlife park, Ashley watched the effect that Tim had on the woman inside the ticket booth. Despite how serious their job was, it was nice to now and then indulge in finding something to be amused about. Tim's looks and the way he affected people were always good for that.

"We're here to see Wayne Medici," Tim said as he held up his badge.

"Wayne … umm…" the woman said as she appeared to glance at something on the interior wall of the booth. "I think … yeah, he's not here today."

"Rostered day off?" Tim asked.

"No, he should be here, but went home early yesterday, saying he wasn't feeling great," the woman said. "Guess he's still feeling under the weather."

"Do you know where he lives?" asked Tim, knowing it was a long shot that anybody would hand out their work colleague's address. Never hurt to give it a go, though. "It's really important that we can talk to him."

For a moment, both agents thought the woman was going to comply and hand them the tiger keeper's home address. Another moment later, she looked more resolved to not give in so easily, no matter how good looking the male agent in front of her was.

"I don't think I can give that out," she said, glancing from one agent to the other. "I'm pretty sure that would get me fired."

"Fair enough," Tim said, plastering on his best charming smile. "Who can give us authority to get that then?"

"Umm … maybe … the boss?" the woman suggested, beginning to blush.

"That would be great. Can you summon him here?" Tim asked, lowering his tone of voice just a little, to the point of depth that seemed to work just that little bit better when trying to get something out of someone. "We don't want you to get into trouble, but this really is important."

"Sure," the woman said before picking up the booth phone and making a quick call. "Mr. Simpson will be out soon."

"Thank you," Tim said, grinning at her again. His charm hadn't worked in that instant. That didn't mean it wouldn't next time.

"Agents," Tim and Ashley heard the park owner, David Simpson, call out from beside the ticket booth.

"Mr. Simpson," both agents said back.

"How can I help you today?" David asked, appearing more than a little bit wary about Bureau agents visiting his park so much in such a small span of time.

"Actually, we were hoping to talk to your tiger keeper again - Wayne Medici," Tim said and saw the park owner nod.

"And?" David asked, surprised. "Did the young lass in the booth not let you in to do that?"

"I'm sorry," Ashley said, confused. "Is he not off work sick today?"

"Oh, is he?" David asked. "I didn't know that. Sorry, I'm only the park owner. I leave all the running of this place to everyone else."

"Yes," Tim said. "Your ticket seller told us that Mr. Medici is off sick, however we do need to speak to him. Would you be willing to authorize us gathering his home address?"

For a long moment, David Simpson looked from one agent to the other, almost as if he had something to hide himself. After Tim and Ashley had granted him the time he seemed to need to make the decision, they saw him finally relax.

"Yes," he said. "Not good practice for any boss to give out details of their staff, I have to say, but if this has something to do with what you've been investigating, I think it best you do talk to him."

"Yes, we do appreciate if you can help us with this. In addition to our investigation, if something has happened to Mr. Medici, we'd like to make sure he is okay," Ashley said, bending their intention just a little bit.

She watched as David Simpson walked to the ticket booth and instructed the young woman inside to bring up the staff list on the computer in front of her. A minute later, David leaned out the ticket booth window and presented the agents with a piece of paper.

"I don't know anything about him being off work sick, but here is what you want," David said. "Generally, he's a good worker, and reliably here for every shift he's rostered on for. Whatever you're needing him for today, you better not take my best tiger keeper."

Tim smiled sadly at the park owner. If he and Ashley were right in their investigation so far, the chances of Wayne Medici returning to tend to Tigger any more were getting slimmer by the hour.

As the two of them climbed into the car to begin their journey to the house where Wayne Medici resided, they remained unaware that in the ticket booth, a young woman who'd seemed demure and innocent, was already on her phone.

# CHAPTER 24

After entering the address into the dashboard GPS, Ashley and Tim made their way across town. Even in the town that might have only just stretched in population to be able to claim the title of a small city, it was clear to see the change in poverty level. As the wildlife park was left further and further behind them, Ashley and Tim could see that either being a tiger keeper didn't pay very well, or the person they were seeking lived a life associated with crime and gangs. They'd thought the neighborhood that Liam Manson lived in had been rough. Even his neighborhood seemed heavenly compared to the part of town that the tiger keeper was reportedly residing in.

When they reached the address they'd been provided with, they were greeted not by a home, but by what many people would call a shack. It looked like a meager attempt at a garden shed, and one that had not only been built long ago, but had also suffered immensely over its lifetime.

Walking around, Ashley and Tim could see no sign of life either inside or outside of the small structure. All in all, the small plot could only be described as a mess, with overgrown grass and weeds, and the shed looking as if it was ready to give up and fall over.

"I'm guessing he's not so sick that he needs to be bedridden," Ashley said when they'd walked around the exterior and peered in the few windows it housed.

"I'll get a trace put on his phone," said Tim. "Maybe it'll give us an indication of where he is."

"Good idea. While we wait for the result of that, let's get back in the car and stay here for a little while," Ashley suggested. "Could be that he's just popped out for something and will be back soon."

"Okay," Tim said before making his way to the passenger door. Before climbing in, he took another good look around the neighborhood. It was a dismal place to live - the shack *and* the street.

When he'd climbed into the car, he turned to Ashley.

"When we met him, I didn't perceive he'd be someone living like this," he said.

"It is surprising," Ashley said. "Then again, aren't they all? These guys that we catch and put away are so much like actors, playing these perfectly innocent roles sometimes. Really, I don't know why they don't stop doing the crime thing and just go off to Hollywood to be movie stars. Better pay."

"Not to mention there's far less likelihood of getting dumped into prison for the rest of your life," Tim added.

Minutes later, his phone rang. As always, the call was short and straight to the point.

"Any luck?" Ashley asked him when she saw him hang up from the call.

"Yep, looks like Medici's phone is currently in a motel - Rose Lee Motel. The guys are now looking to see when Medici last made contact with Rayna Cunningham as well," Tim said as he began to enter the address into the GPS. "One hour south, this thing is saying."

"Cool," said Ashley. "Let's go and see what this guy has to say this time."

"It's an hour away," Tim said. "I'll put through a request for the local PD to go to the motel now, just in case Medici gets wind of us being on his tail and he does another runner."

Under an hour later, they entered the small town that the motel resided in. Briefly calling into the police station closest to the Rose Lee Motel, Ashley and Tim were greeted by the station Chief.

"Your guy appears to be inside the room that he rented," he said. "I've got men covering the front and the rear, just in case he bolts, but they haven't seen any movement from the room as yet. Manager is ready to give you a key to get in, should you want to use it."

"Alright, well, thank you," Ashley said as she shook his hand. "Time for us to pay Mr. Medici a visit."

On arrival at the motel, it was easy for Tim and Ashley to see local law enforcement sitting in wait, even if they were in plain clothing. Once the agents were told which room Medici was in, and had met the motel manager, they moved subtly to the door and knocked.

"Mr. Medici!" Tim called out on hearing no reply or sensing any movement inside. "This is Special Agents Moore and Power. We need to talk to you."

Still hearing nothing, Tim summoned to the motel manager to move forward with unlocking the door. When the door was opened, Tim and Ashley stepped inside with a further officer behind them, prepared for any possibility.

At first glance, it looked like Wayne Medici was nowhere to be seen. After taking a few steps into the bathroom, Tim pulling back the shower curtain over the bath produced a different result.

# CHAPTER 25

"Well, well, well," Tim said, surprised by the relaxed effort of the man in front of him to hide. "Got something to hide, Mr. Medici?"

"I'm not telling you anything!" Wayne said, trying unsuccessfully to remain out of Tim's reach in the bathtub. "I love her. I won't tell you nothing!"

"Hmm," said Tim as he grabbed Wayne by the shoulders and yanked him out of the tub. He wasn't surprised to hear the man's vocabulary sound so different to how it had been when they'd previously met him. It was just another way that some criminals were - able to act with the most polite and relaxed manner ... until they were caught out in their lies. "Well, that is certainly your right, however as things are right now, you could go down for this entire crime. Is she really worth doing that for?"

"I know my rights," Wayne said as the cuffs went on. "You can't charge me with anything!"

"Such a tantrum you throw, when all we wanted to do was ask you some more questions," Tim said as he gladly handed Medici over to one of the local cops. "Take him to the precinct and let him get comfortable. We'll be along to ask him some questions shortly."

"He's much more spirited now than he was when we first questioned him, I have to say," Tim said to Ashley when they got into the car.

"Nice that he's pretty much admitted that he and Rayna were in this together, though," Ashley said. "What do you think? Go back and grab her while she might still be in town?"

"An hour's drive back," said Tim, grinning. "Yeah, probably won't hurt for him to stew in a local cell for a few hours."

# CHAPTER 26

On the way north again, Tim and Ashley were both thoughtful. Even though they'd had to use the help of their peers to find out where Wayne had gone to, it had still seemed a little too easy to catch up to him. Something about that bugged both agents.

"Do you think he had opportunity to warn her?" Ashley asked before they arrived back in town.

"Maybe," Tim replied. "He had enough foresight to get himself out of town, so it would only have taken a quick phone call or text to let her know we might also be on her tail as well."

"Hmm," Ashley muttered, not sure what was making her feel like her gut was leading her in another direction.

Regardless of the sliver of doubt she experienced, she focused on making her way to the house of Rayna Cunningham once more. For a moment, she thought about Rayna's neighbor, Bob Thompson. Would he miss her when she was behind bars? Would he have anyone else that he could lean on if he needed assistance with anything? The answers to those questions were irrelevant to their investigation, but it was still something that remained in Ashley's thoughts until she was distracted from it.

When Tim's phone rang, they were almost at the street where Rayna and Bob resided. Part way through the conversation, Ashley saw Tim signal for her to stop the car. Uncertain what was happening, Ashley carefully veered into a parking stop on the side of the road and waited for him to finish up his call.

"We have to put this on hold," Tim said, not trying to hide the excitement he felt inside. "That was the computer forensics guys again. They finally got through their next level of … *whatever* it is that they have to break through."

"Okay, great, but what are you talking about?" Ashley asked in frustration. "We need to get Rayna before she skips…"

"Not yet," Tim insisted. "The guys dug deeper into the money skimming."

"And?" Ashley asked, realizing she'd almost forgotten about the issue of the money that been stolen from the local power company.

"They've been monitoring the account that the money goes into," said Tim.

"The one that's in Rayna's name…" Ashley said, asking for clarification.

"That's just it - it's in her name, but she hasn't been accessing it at all," said Tim, grinning.

In such times, Ashley felt a familiar desire to punch her partner for dragging details out so much.

"Tim!" she demanded and saw him chuckle before growing serious again.

"The account was accessed two hours ago - from the Templeton house computer," Tim finally said. "We need to go there."

"Steven Templeton's finally showing us his intentions for him and Rayna?" Ashley asked as she started the car.

"Looks that way," Tim said, feeling rather chuffed that he might have been right all along.

"How are we going to approach this?" Ashley asked a few minutes later as she considered all of the residents of the household they were approaching. "Kids might be there. I'd rather not arrest their father for attempted murder in front of them."

"How about let's just go and ask questions, see what Steven Templeton has to say, and take it from there."

# CHAPTER 27

On approach to the Templeton property, the absence of Steven Templeton's car was immediately noticeable.

"You think he's done a runner as well?" Ashley asked before they climbed out of the car.

"Maybe, or he could be just at work. Only one way to find out," said Tim, hastening his steps to get to the door.

Although both agents expected there might be no reply, it was only a minute or so before the door opened and, in front of them, stood the person they were seeking.

"Mr. Templeton, we have some more questions for you," Tim said.

Watching Steven Templeton's face, Tim saw alarm, but to his surprise, he and Ashley were quietly welcomed into the home regardless.

"We thought you must have been out," Ashley said and saw Steven's look of questioning. "Your car isn't out there."

"Oh. No," Steven Templeton replied. "Alana had to go and get some groceries from the supermarket. She always takes mine when she's going to do a grocery shop far bigger than we actually need."

The tone of the words weren't lost on Ashley. What she'd heard when Steven had spoken was a high level of dissatisfaction about his wife.

"You sound..." Ashley started to say before

seeing the look that he gave her. At first, it was harsh, almost as if he expected her to accuse him of something. She was relieved to see it then soften.

"Sorry. When I got home from my shift an hour ago, she grabbed my car keys and took off without hardly a word," Steven elaborated. "It's been like this since … well, since she found out about the affair. Whatever ground we'd managed to mutually cover to get things back on track, it's definitely been ripped up again now."

"We'd like to ask you about your home computer," Tim said, wanting to bypass the heartfelt stories he anticipated might follow if he allowed Steven Templeton to continue on the path of conversation he'd embarked upon.

"Computer?" Steven asked, looking up at Tim. "That one?" he then asked, pointing to a desktop set up in a discreet corner of the living area. "What about it?"

"It could be useful to our investigation," Tim said.

"Our *computer*?" Steven asked, confused. "Our computer has something to do with a *tiger* coming to our home? Are you *mad*?"

"Were you on it two hours ago, Mr. Templeton?" Ashley asked to gather confirmation.

"No," Steven said, shaking his head. "Like I said, I got home from a shift at the hospital an hour ago - give or take five or ten minutes. And even if I had been here then - which I wasn't - I have no need to *use* a computer. Hate the things."

"You're a surgeon," Tim said and saw Steven nod. "Don't you have to use computers for your work? Write reports or something?"

"No! I avoid them like the plague whenever I

can," said Steven. "I dictate everything and I hand it to whichever surgical administrator is on duty at the time. They transcribe it, prepare a report, which they then print off and hand to me in the form of paper for checking. That's how I've always done it, and I've never had any desire to change it. As far as I'm concerned, those things have taken over the world far too much. I cringe when I see Alana or the girls sitting at it. What happened to kids getting out in the sunshine?"

As he spoke, Tim and Ashley looked at one another. They'd focused on Steven. There was another possibility.

"Is Alana due back soon, do you think?" Tim asked.

"I … I don't know," Steven said, sounding defeated. "She's changed…"

"Changed how?" asked Ashley.

"I guess how any woman would change when they found out that their husband had cheated on them," Steven said. "It's not surprising, but it makes things so uncomfortable now." Glancing at the wall clock, he frowned.

"Are you able to call her and ask her to come home?" Ashley suggested. "We'd like to speak to her as well."

Without answering with words, Steven pulled out his phone and dialed Alana's number. Everyone was surprised when the sound of a phone ringing came from the kitchen.

Standing up, Steven walked toward it slowly. He'd been so frustrated by the cold shoulder he'd received when he'd arrived home, that he'd sat on the sofa and not moved after the interaction. He hadn't noticed his wife's phone sitting on the kitchen bench.

"My wife never goes anywhere without her phone," he said as he picked it up and turned to face the agents. "Has something happened to my wife?"

"How ... was Alana when you saw her, Mr. Templeton?" Tim asked, curious about the man's demeanor.

"I just told you," Steven replied, with a tinge of annoyance evident in his voice. "We crossed paths, she grabbed my keys, and she left. She's been like that pretty much all the time since ... that last time you were here."

"Hmm," said Tim, his mind working. "I'm just going to step outside to make a call," he added, glancing at Ashley and seeing her nod at him.

Outside, he called the office to ask if they could confirm anything about Steven's computer skills. Within a couple of minutes, he had received a call saying that the team had briefly talked to the hospital and done a search to see if Steven Templeton had ever done any computer courses of any kind.

"We'll keep digging but for now, there's nothing that we can see that would indicate that he's got anything more than the most basic computer knowledge at all," the team member said to Tim. "Ward at the hospital confirmed that he does do his reports in an old-fashioned way, with a dictaphone and paper printouts. Person I spoke to was pretty adamant that Steven Templeton is a pain in the ass, with the way he refuses to just sit at a computer and do things the same way as everyone else in their department."

"Okay, thanks," Tim replied. He was about to hang up when the team member spoke again.

"Different story for his *wife*, however," he said.

"Alana Templeton?" Tim asked.

"Yep. You name it, she's done the course in it," the team member continued. "Website design, coding, database manipulation … all the ones she's done are legit courses, but there are some in the extensive list that are pretty in-depth. Definitely not something a complete amateur could easily do."

"Hmm. Is there anything on that list that could transfer to … hacking into business systems?" Tim asked.

"I can't confirm that," said the team member. "But if you're asking me if someone with this level of computer knowledge could easily pick up the *skills* in how to hack systems, then yes. She has done a lot of these courses, and she's passed every one with flying colors. Nothing less than an A on any paper."

"But they aren't directly related to anything criminal…"

"Well, no, of course not, but if you're looking for a hacker, to a degree at least, she could probably do it. The most important skill I can see that she has, is the ability to easily learn and adapt to whatever's happening inside a computer, including working remotely to dig into other computers."

"Okay, thanks," Tim said, surprised but grateful.

As he walked back inside, his mind was disturbed.

"Mr. Templeton," he said when he re-entered the living room. "What would you say Alana's level of computer knowledge would be?"

"Alana?" Steven asked. "Average, I guess. She's on the damn thing enough, but whenever I've seen her using it, she's just playing some mindless card game or other. I know she used to use them in her work for writing notes and doing research, but she doesn't need to do any of that now - not while she's staying at home anyway. Why?"

Tim took a moment to think about his current suspicion. As much as it looked possible, was it in any way probable? The entire possibility seemed absolutely absurd.

"Look, what is this really about?" Steven asked when he'd received no answer to his question. "No, I don't use computers if I can avoid it. Yes, Alana does. What does any of that have to do with someone bringing that bloody tiger to our home?"

"Mr. Templeton, on the two occasions when Tigger was found here, you were doing your charity golf events?" Tim asked and saw Steven nod. "Both times?"

"Yes, as I've already told you, I do that one day every month," Steven said, his tone further indicating that his patience was obviously being tested. "And, yes, both instances of this happening were days when I was doing the charity golf event."

"And who knows that you do this every month?" asked Tim.

"Lots of people!" Steven replied, the growing frustration evident in his voice and facial expression.

"Yes, but who always knows of the *exact* day that you'll be doing it?" Tim asked.

"I have to take leave from my work on that one day, so most of the people in my workplace," said Steven. "My golf-playing friends who also take part in the event each month. My *wife*."

"And Rayna?" Ashley asked, not sure where Tim's questioning was going, but reading that whatever he'd learned from the phone call he'd made, it was important.

"No, of course not," said Steven, shaking his head. "As I've said before, I haven't seen Rayna for years - not since we stopped seeing each other. When I was seeing her, I wasn't doing these events. There's no way she'd even know that I do them - not that I can think of anyway. I told you that she and I are over, and have been for a long time."

"You started doing these charity golf events since you broke the relationship off," Ashley said.

"Yes," Steven replied. "Why do you keep bringing Rayna up? Does she have something to do with that animal turning up here? Does she have something to do with Alana..." he began to ask before unconsciously glancing at the clock again. "She doesn't usually take this long to do the shopping. Where is my wife?"

"She'd never take more than an hour to go to the supermarket?" Ashley asked.

"Maybe, but I don't see why," said Steven. "I know other people can easily spend a couple of hours shopping for groceries, but Alana hates crowds. When she goes to any kind of shop, we always have to get in, get what we need, and then leave again. She isn't someone who likes lurking and taking her time. When it comes to grocery shops, she makes a list and she sticks to it..."

As Steven suddenly stood and walked to the kitchen, Ashley and Tim watched him.

"Is something wrong, Mr. Templeton?" Ashley asked.

"The list..." Steven started to say as he reached out to touch a piece of paper on the refrigerator door. When he turned back to look at the agents again, they could see panic on his face. "The list is still here..." he said and then paused, confusion clear in his face. "If she didn't take her phone, and she didn't take the grocery list ... then where *is* she?" he asked yet again.

"Mr. Templeton, thinking back to the days that the tiger escaped," Tim began to ask. "Can you take us through your movements on those mornings?"

Although he initially looked surprised and somewhat annoyed at the question, Steven answered.

"The events go all day long, starting at 8.30 am," he said. "Because Alana always seems stressed in the mornings, I take the girls to school whenever I can - if I'm not already in surgery. On the golf charity event days, Bonnie and Dani like helping to set up the event, so we all get up extra early and I take them with me to the golf course. They have a good time, helping set up tables and any outside shelters that we might be setting up. When it's time for them to go to school, I drop them there."

"You have no need to come home again then, before the event begins?" Tim asked.

"No," said Steven. "Me and the girls always get out of here early so that Alana can get on with her day, without us being in her way."

"So it's always her and your son who are left here by themselves early on those mornings?" asked Ashley.

"Yes," Steven replied. "We're usually out of here pretty early anyway, but that day every month, we leave pretty much just before sunrise. Like I say, Dani and Bonnie like coming along and helping out. It's something different for them to do. Sometimes they try and use it as an excuse to get out of school," he added, quietly chuckling even while his eyes looked almost tearful. "They know that isn't going to happen. Education is important. That's one of the things … one of the *few* things … that Alana and I do still agree on."

Ashley and Tim watched as Steven returned to his seat, sat down with his head in his hands, and exhibited signs of truly feeling concerned - or defeated.

Tim's phone ringing interrupted the silence. When he'd excused himself and stepped outside again to answer the call, his attention was grabbed by one of the head office guys calling.

"You asked us to look into when Wayne Medici last called Rayna Cunningham?" the voice asked.

"Yep," Tim said, surprised that he'd briefly forgotten the request. He'd seen call logs that indicated it had been a while. At the time when he'd made the request, he'd also hoped that further delving might reveal that the calls hadn't actually stopped at all.

"Well, as far as that question goes, it's been two months since those two had contact, *but…*" the voice said. "Medici has been in contact with someone else associated with this case."

"Who?" Tim asked.

"Alana Templeton," the voice said. "Those two have been in contact a lot over the past eight months."

"When was the most recent contact?" asked Tim, beginning to feel dread in his gut.

"She tried calling him eighty minutes ago, but it doesn't look like he answered the call. Last time they actually spoke was about four and a half hours ago, and that was a decent call, lasting almost half an hour," said the voice. After a long pause of silence, they continued. "Was there anything else you need us to investigate right now? Put a trace on her phone?"

"No," Tim said, surprised by the revelation that he and Ashley hadn't even considered as a possibility. "The phone is here with us at their home, so no point in doing that. Thanks. If we think of anything else you might be able to find out for us, I'll call you."

When he walked back into the living area again, Tim felt like he was in disbelief. What he'd just learned meant an array of things might have happened that just seemed highly unlikely.

"Mr. Templeton," he said when he sat down again. "Is there any chance that your wife is having - or recently has had - an affair?"

"What?" Steven asked, horrified. "What … why … how dare you!"

"Please just answer the question," Tim said.

"No, of course not!" Steven replied.

"You sound surprised by the possibility," Ashley said. "Yet you have admitted that *you* had an affair that lasted for two years - two years, during which your wife had no idea about it."

"Yes but…" Steven started to argue before taking a moment to really consider the possibility. "She wouldn't." He paused for longer. "Why? And with who?" he asked. "*Who?*"

"We're still investigating this, Mr. Templeton," said Tim. "However, I think there might be a possibility that your wife hasn't been entirely truthful."

"About what?" Steven asked.

"About … almost everything that she's told us,"

Tim said.

"What? She didn't make up there being a tiger here, which is what you came here for in the first place," said Steven. "No, the vet came here and put it to sleep and then took it back to the park … you don't think that she made it up - and he's gone along with the story? It's a story that isn't true?"

"No, not at all," said Tim. "The tiger did get out of the park, and it was here. The local PD have confirmed that. Your wife didn't make up that story."

"Then … what are you saying?" Steven asked.

"Is … is there any chance that your wife … organized all of this?" Tim asked, hardly believing himself that it could be an option. "That she was the one behind it all?"

As Tim and Ashley watched, Steven stood up and began to pace the room. As he did, Ashley glanced at Tim. He had information that he hadn't shared with her, but she trusted where and why his odd line of questioning had led down the particular path that it had.

"You can't be saying…" Steven finally said as he stopped pacing and faced the agents. "You can't mean … that Alana planned for that tiger to come to our house … while she was here … and our *son* was here…? Please tell me that isn't what you're implying."

"Unfortunately, it's a possibility that we can't yet rule out," said Tim. "She has been communicating a great deal with a man who is associated with the tiger. She's also been in touch with him within the last few hours."

"But … she would bring something like that to our home, and near our son?" Steven asked in obvious disbelief. "It could have ... it could have *killed* her. It could have killed *Tony*."

Tim nodded but waited in silence for the man before him to fully process the possibility.

"I can't believe this," Steven finally said. "Sorry, but you must have gotten your wires crossed somewhere. You must have. That cannot be a real possibility. Someone would have to be *insane* to do that."

"It *is* only a theory for now, Mr. Templeton," Tim said. "As soon as we can speak to Alana, she'll be able to better explain what's been going on, I'm sure."

Steven glanced at the clock once again. More time had passed, and still his wife wasn't home. Her phone was in the kitchen. There was no way to call her to ask her what was truth and what was fiction.

"What do I do?" he asked. "How do I find out where Alana is?"

"I think it best that you remain here in case she comes home soon," Tim said as he stood. "We will go to the supermarket she uses, and see if we can locate her there. I'm sure there will be a logical explanation for all of this," he said even though he didn't believe there could be.

"Very well," Steven said, remaining where he was as Ashley and Tim walked out.

"Wow, you really know how to throw a curve ball into questioning. What was that all about?" Ashley asked when they were in the car and on their way to the supermarket that Steven had said Alana always went to.

"Guys from head office called," Tim replied. "It isn't Rayna that Medici's been in contact with all this time - it's Alana Templeton."

Ashley had suspected something like that when Tim had been inside talking to Steven. Hearing it come from Tim's mouth in such simple terms was still a shock.

"You think they've been having an affair?" she asked.

"Can't say," said Tim. "The guys could only see at short notice that there'd been calls between Alana and Medici. There were no text messages to read so we don't know what was discussed between them. Most recently, they talked a few hours ago. Since then, she must have tried to reach him before she left the house, but he didn't answer."

"Because he's locked up," surmised Ashley.

"Right," Tim agreed. "His phone will be currently confiscated, so I don't know what Alana will be thinking since he didn't answer her call. Doesn't really matter since she left her phone at the house, unless she's going to use a burner or something, but the guys looking into the call log didn't see another number since she last called him before leaving here."

"Wow," Ashley said. "So, what you're thinking is that, somehow, Alana Templeton influenced the tiger keeper to get the tiger to her home when she was there with her infant … and she went outside in front of it, and had her infant within reach of it? She *made* that happen?"

Seeing Tim nod made Ashley shudder.

"Shit, that's … what the hell *is* that?" she asked. She'd seen a lot of crap parents over her time as an agent, but putting one's infant in front of a big cat was beyond crazy.

"I don't know," said Tim. "All I can think is that there's something seriously wrong with her if she did this intentionally."

"And *why?*" Ashley pondered. "What was the point of it?"

"That, I guess we'll find out when we track her down," Tim said. "And that's the next challenge - where exactly *is* Alana Templeton right now?"

"You're not buying the grocery shopping story that she told her husband?" asked Ashley.

"That's something we can't confirm or rule out right now," said Tim. "Supermarket is just up here. Let's see if we can spot Steven Templeton's car."

Looking around the vast carpark, neither agent expected to see the car there, so neither was surprised that it wasn't amongst the sea of vehicles.

"There's no other way for her to drive from here to the house, so we can't have missed her if she was here and is now on her way home," Tim said. "I'll put a BOLO out for the car," he continued as he pulled out his phone.

"Okay, let's do a quick drive around just in case she is here in town but doing something else," said Ashley. "If she's been talking to Wayne Medici as recently as a few hours ago, she might already be on her way to that motel that he's already been caught at."

"True," Tim agreed. "BOLO is out for Steven's car so hopefully that'll yield some results soon enough."

"I just can't believe that someone - a *mother* - would do something like that," Ashley said, focusing on the possibility. "Does she not like her kid or something?"

"If it was just something like that, I don't think she'd put herself in danger's way, Ash," Tim said. "And she could have stood back and let the tiger get her son, if that was the case. Either way, there definitely has to be something really off about this woman."

"She did seem vague and confused, that first time that we met and interviewed her," said Ashley. "Steven also mentioned that she's been confused at times, seeming to not know that she was going to do something that she'd previously said she would. Maybe there's some kind of dual personality going on or something."

"Who knows," Tim said as he continued to watch up and down each street they entered. "It's certainly a strange thing, and a first of its kind for me. I don't get it any more than you do. Let's see if she opens up and says anything once we catch up with her."

"You sound pretty sure that we will," Ashley said, glancing at him, and catching him smiling at her.

"No doubt about that, Special Agent Ashley Power," Tim said, grinning. "No matter how far or wide they run, we always find them."

Although Ashley knew his words weren't true - there were plenty of criminals who'd escaped law enforcement over the years - she smiled back and didn't reply. They didn't always get the bad guys, but she maintained hope that on their current case, they would.

# CHAPTER 28

After scouring as many obvious places and locations that Alana Templeton might have been at if she hadn't intentionally left town, Ashley began the drive south.

"I wonder if Mr. Medici will feel more like talking, now that he's had a few hours behind bars," Ashley said. "Works for some people."

"Not enough, unfortunately," Tim said. "He sounded pretty resolute about not saying anything that will incriminate the woman he was talking about."

"Who we now believe is Alana Templeton," Ashley added.

"Yeah, hopefully we've got that right," said Tim. "The guys at head office didn't see any contact between Medici and Rayna Cunningham in recent times, so I'm pretty confident she didn't have anything to do with any of this."

"But what about the money skimming?" Ashley asked. "You think that Alana did that too? Is that why you were asking her husband about her skills in computer use?"

"Yeah, there's a really strong record of her having completed a lot of advanced computer courses that the IT guys think would have provided her with the skills to hack into systems," Tim said. "It could have been her that did everything."

"And the life insurance policy that was taken out

in her name?" Ashley pondered. "Alana took that out on herself and made it look like it was Steven who did it?"

"Quite possibly, yes," said Tim. "The computer forensics guys should be able to figure that out in time."

"But if she was that good at hacking, why would she have needed Liam Manson?" asked Ashley. "Big risk to bring someone like him into the plan, when Alana could have just done it all herself."

"Maybe her skills don't extend quite that far," Tim suggested. "Hopefully we'll have some answers soon. Let's see what Mr. Medici has to say about all of this. Alana making it all happen seems like such an extreme … not to mention *weird* … possibility."

On arrival at the police precinct building, they were greeted by the station Chief again.

"Is he talking?" Tim asked and saw the Chief shake his head. "Not surprising at all. Can we see him?"

"Yep. Come through to this interrogation room and we'll bring him in to join you shortly," the Chief said before leaving them alone in the stark room with only a table and a few chairs.

When Wayne Medici entered the room, it was easy to see that, in contrast to the fairly civil aura he'd given off when Ashley and Tim had first met him, his current body language said he was going to be anything but cooperative.

"Seems you and your lady have been up to some no good, Mr. Medici," Tim began as he started to analyze every visible movement of Wayne Medici's facial muscles. "Was it all worth it? Being involved with setting a tiger onto a mother and her child seems likely to be a basis for attempted murder."

"I ain't got nothing to tell you," Wayne said, his voice betraying a sliver of concern inside of him.

"Really? *Nothing* to tell us?" Ashley asked. "There have been some real twists in this case, but you seem to be at the centre of them. First, there's the issue of pretending to be someone called Andrew - the boyfriend of Rayna Cunningham. Then, there's the issue of using your access to the park to facilitate the stealing of a protected animal from its home. Add to that the processes involved to get the animal to a home where it could have killed a woman and an infant."

"And to top all of that off, you're looking like you'll be held responsible for over a million dollars having been stolen from the local electricity corporation," Tim added. He hoped that something that he and Ashley might have said, might prompt the guy in front of them to speak. His hope was rewarded.

"*I* never took any money!" Wayne exclaimed, appearing genuinely surprised by the allegation.

"And yet, that is all associated with the tiger being delivered to the Templeton's home…"

"No," Wayne said, looking confused. "What are you talking about? That has nothing to do with the plan…"

As both agents watched him, they saw his resolve begin to fade slightly.

"Perhaps you might like to tell us what exactly the plan was, so we can have a better idea, and don't charge you with something you aren't responsible for," Tim said.

"I … I just had to pretend to be interested in that Rayna chick," Wayne finally began to say after a lengthy period of silent contemplation. "That was all I was asked to do. That has nothing to do with any money."

"Okay, let's say we believe you," Ashley said. "Tell us more about pretending to be Rayna's … boyfriend? Who told you to do that?"

"I'm not naming anyone," Wayne said as he sat back and crossed his arms in an attempt to look defiant. "I already told you that."

"Fair enough," said Tim. "If you're willing to take all the blame for all of this, that's your call. For now, how about you tell us *why* you pretended to be Rayna's boyfriend. What was the point of that?"

"To get close to her," Wayne replied.

"And?" asked Ashley. "What then? *Why* get close to Rayna?"

"To … to figure out if she had a history with a guy," Wayne replied quietly.

As Tim watched, he felt good inside. In their job, some of the people they interviewed were staunch enough to stick to their story of innocence, no matter what they were subjected to. He was glad that, in front of him, was someone he was sure was going to tell them an entire story in no time at all. It didn't happen often, but on a rare occasion, it was just how things went.

"Steven Templeton," he said and immediately saw the reaction he was hoping to see. "You invested several months into pretending to like Rayna just to find out … if she'd had a relationship with him? Seems like a pretty extreme effort to go to."

"So you've got some kind of romantic flame for Steven Templeton?" Ashley asked, keeping her face straight while internally expecting an enjoyable response to the question. She wasn't disappointed with how the man facing her reacted.

"No!" Wayne exclaimed with force behind that one word. "It was … look, the time I spent with Rayna was alright. I liked her. She was an okay chick."

"Even though you were using her for information," Tim suggested.

"Yeah. So? Everybody uses everybody for something," Wayne said, his tone defensive.

"Do you love her?" Ashley asked.

"Rayna? No, of course not," said Wayne. "Don't get me wrong. She's a nice enough lady, but she was just a means to an end."

"With the end being?" asked Tim.

"Knowing if she'd been involved with Templeton," Wayne replied.

"Hmm," Ashley said. "But just to be clear, Mr. Medici, when I asked if you love her, I wasn't asking in past tense. I didn't ask if you *loved* her - Rayna. I ask if you *love* her - the woman you're doing all of this for."

For a long time, silence lay across the room as Wayne Medici looked down at his lap, appearing to contemplate his options.

"She is everything to me," he finally said, his voice almost a whisper.

"Everything?" Tim and saw Wayne nod. "You really think she's worth going to prison for? She's worth giving up your freedom for?"

"Do you think she loves you?" Ashley dared to ask.

"She does love me!" Wayne said with passion. "She's told me I'm her soul mate. We're meant to be together forever."

"And yet she isn't here," Ashley said. "If she

loved you, wouldn't she be here, doing whatever she could to get you out of here? If she loved you, would she really let you take the rap for all of this?"

"Do you think she does love you, Wayne, or is there a chance that she just used you to get what she wanted, knowing that you would do exactly what you're doing now - stepping up to take the blame so that she can get away with her role in this?" Tim asked, taking a moment to nudge open the small crack of uncertainty he could see on the face in front of him. "Would that make you happy - to know that you gave everything up and went to prison for her? Will it make you happy when you see that she won't come and visit you once you're put behind bars? Once you've done your part and she's gotten away with it, you know there's a good chance you'll never see her again."

"You're wrong!" Wayne said. His voice sounded like he wanted to show he was strong. It also sounded like he was beginning to fear exactly what the agents were suggesting might be the case. "She loves me as much as I love her."

Ashley and Tim sat still, remained quiet, and waited. They'd interviewed hundreds of people throughout their careers. They both could see that there were telltale signs that Wayne Medici was about to crack. So far, they hadn't suggested a name for who they believed the woman was that he was protecting. That information, they wanted him to give up himself.

"You have a chance to tell us where she is, Mr. Medici," Ashley said as one last plea. "Let us bring her in. If she loves you like you say she does, she'll be glad to know where you are. She'll be glad to know you're safe."

Wayne Medici glanced at Ashley. He had to concede that she was an attractive woman, and that was one thing that he did love in life - women. If he took responsibility for everything that had happened, and was put behind bars for the rest of his life, he'd possibly never see another woman ever again. Did he want that? On reflection, even knowing how much he loved the woman in his life - his soul mate - he didn't think he *was* ready to give all women up, or his freedom if he could help it.

"She was going to meet me at the motel where you picked me up," he finally said. "I don't know if she went there or not. She was going to make contact with me again when she was on her way, but I haven't got my phone…"

Ashley didn't hesitate to leave the room and retrieve his phone from the belongings being held.

"Check your voicemail messages," she said as she held the phone up.

Taking care to hold it securely, but close enough for him to be able to dial his voicemail number, Ashley watched over his shoulder to make sure he wasn't doing anything else. When the call messages started playing, they heard exactly what they wanted to.

"Wayne, Darling," a woman's familiar voice rang out across the small room. "I've got the rental car, and I'm on my way now to meet you. I'm booked into the motel, but I've asked for a different room from you. You know there's only one room I could be in, and that's the one we first met in. You remember it, don't you, Darling? I'm on my way there, and I'll be there with you soon. I left my regular phone behind, so make sure you call me back on this number instead."

When the message ended, they heard the standard closing 'you have no more messages'.

"Which room?" Tim asked. Although he saw Wayne look hesitant, it took surprisingly little time before he appeared to change his mind about withholding whatever information he was holding onto. "*Which room?*"

"Room 35," Wayne finally said.

"So she's in a rental car," Tim pondered. "Why?"

"Knows people would identify her car, I'm guessing," said Wayne. "You heard the message she left me. Sounds like she checked into a different room at the motel so we wouldn't be associated together."

"Is that what she wanted, do you mean?" Tim asked. "It was *her* idea that you have separate spaces?"

"Yeah, well, I haven't spoken to her since I left town," Wayne replied. "Whatever she's doing now, she's doing it on her own since you've got me locked up here."

"And you don't think it's a coincidence that you were located so easily, but she's still free?" asked Ashley, hoping they were nudging Wayne closer to not being quite so loyal to whoever it was that he was protecting.

"Maybe," Wayne said in almost a whisper.

"Good. Now, for accuracy in our records, tell us the name of this mystery woman who put you up to all this," Ashley dared to ask, hoping they'd gotten everything right so far.

"Alana," Wayne finally disclosed, his facial expression conveying that maybe his loyalty had changed from protecting her, to protecting only himself. "Alana Templeton."

# CHAPTER 29

With a couple of officers from the local police department as support, Ashley and Tim made their way back to the motel and assembled around the front and back of room 35. It still surprised Ashley that Alana could be the one responsible for everything that had happened - especially with her having put herself and her child in such danger - but they had to assume that everything was panning out that way.

"Alana Templeton!" Tim called out as he banged on the door. "This is Special Agent Moore. Open up!"

For a long time, it seemed that there might not be anyone in the room. Before the agents and officers needed to take action to open the door themselves, Alana revealed herself.

"Agents..." she said as if surprised. "I ... what brings you here?" she went on to ask, her voice almost as sweet as what Ashley could assume an angel would sound like.

"Mrs. Templeton, we'd like you to come to the police station with us," Tim said as he indirectly guided her outside.

"I ... I don't understand," Alana said, even though she willingly began to walk with Tim toward one of the officer's patrol cars. "Has something happened to Steven?"

"Steven?" Ashley asked her with a sliver of

sarcasm in her voice. "You ask about just your husband? Not your kids? Or perhaps they aren't as important to you."

Although Ashley expected any mother to vehemently argue with that statement, she found she wasn't so surprised that Alana remained silent instead. Of all the aspects of the case that had surprised Ashley, that was the one that deeply saddened her.

# CHAPTER 30

Settled into the police station interrogation room, Tim and Ashley took their time to observe Alana Templeton's facial expressions and body language. Whatever she honestly thought about inside her head, both agents could see that she was able to do an amazing job of conveying the role of a victim. Nothing about her demeanor signaled to them that she thought she'd done anything wrong.

"You've led us on quite a goose chase," Tim said, demanding Alana's attention. "All these theatrics - including claiming a tiger went to your home and almost killed you and your son..."

"That tiger *did* come to our home and try to attack us!" Alana argued right on cue. "Do you think I made that up?"

"Actually, no. There are enough witnesses to that, for us to not doubt that it did happen," said Tim. "The surprise has been learning that not only did you want it to happen, but you *made* it happen."

"Why would you do that, Alana?" Ashley asked. "Put yourself at risk like that? Put *Tony* at risk like that? What could possibly have motivated you to do that?"

Silence ensued as she and Tim watched the woman they faced. Both agents hoped that Alana would just come clean about everything. Instead, she remained still, occasionally looking up at them, but then quickly returning her gaze downwards.

"We want to understand," Ashley said softly. When no response came, she moved forward into her job of questioning. "Alright, well, perhaps we can start by you telling us what your involvement is with Wayne Medici."

Although the name appeared to contribute to a slight shift in body stance in Alana, she still didn't speak.

"He tells us that you love him," Ashley said. "That you've loved him for quite a while."

"I love my husband!" Alana finally said, sitting up taller and seeming to wake up, ready to face whatever fight was about to begin.

"So you say, but then where do things stand between you and Mr. Medici?" Ashley asked.

"He gave your name up, you know," Tim said, trying a different tactic. "Didn't hesitate in saying that everything that we've been investigating - the tiger escaping and going to your home, and the issue with the money skimming..."

"Rayna fucking Cunningham," Alana said under her breath at the mention of the money. When she got no response from Ashley or Tim after speaking, she raised her head and looked straight at them. "Everything was fine until she made her way into my marriage. They deserve everything coming to them."

"They - who?" Ashley asked. "I can see that you're angry. Who exactly are you angry at?"

"Who do you think?" Alana asked with contempt in her voice, her tone changing completely. "He married me. He was supposed to be with me and *only* me for the rest of our lives. Till death do us part. That's what our vows said."

"And you *are* still married..." Ashley stated,

wondering where Alana's strange logic was going to go.

"He left me for her - maybe not physically left, but his heart left," Alana said. "He thought I didn't know. Of course I knew! One minute, he was my loving husband. The next … he had no attention to give anymore. Work, work, work, he kept saying to me. Lies. All lies. Yes, he worked. But how much of the time, when he said he was working, was he actually with her? How much?!"

"Right," Tim said, nodding. "So you wanted to … do what? Hurt Steven? How would all of this do that?"

"Loves his kids more than he loves me," Alana said.

"*His* kids?" asked Ashley. "Alana, they're your kids too…"

"No!" Alana exclaimed. "He wanted kids, so I gave them to him. He always loved them more than he ever loved me."

"Okay, perhaps we can backtrack a bit," Tim said, eager to figure out *how* everything had happened, more than why. "How long have you known Wayne Medici?"

"I met him briefly a few years back," Alana answered.

"Okay," said Ashley. "When you represented his cousin in court?"

"Yes," Alana replied. "Nick - his cousin - told me about how Wayne was a tiger keeper at the park."

"Okay, but that was a few years back, you said?"

"I … I forgot about him but then … I … I … Steven pulled away from me," said Alana. "He was going to ask for a divorce, I was sure of it."

"So you wanted to make sure that didn't happen," Tim suggested and saw Alana nod.

"I wanted to make him not want to leave me. He said those vows to me. He should have stuck to them! He didn't," Alana said. "I remembered about the tiger keeper and thought..." she continued before her words drifted off to silence.

"Help us to understand, Alana," Tim said. "What exactly did you hope was going to happen if you got the tiger into your home?"

"I'd make them pay," Alana said in a tone that indicated she thought that was the most obvious answer there could be.

"How, exactly?" asked Ashley, still in disbelief about how different the woman in front of her was appearing, compared to the times they'd met her inside the Templeton home.

"They needed to pay!" Alana said, not seeming to have understood what was being asked.

"Do you love Wayne Medici?" Tim asked.

"No!" Alana replied. "I ... he was needed for this, that's all."

"And him pretending to be someone else and spending time with Rayna Cunningham?" asked Ashley. The grin she received from Alana Templeton in that moment was so evil-looking that Ashley felt a shiver go through her.

"Wanted to make that bitch believe someone loved her, and she did believe it," Alana said. "Lapped it up like a cat with a bowl of cream put in front of it."

"Just like you wanted to make Mr. Medici believe that you loved him?" asked Tim.

"He was useful, that's all," said Alana, smiling. "Idiot thought I was going to divorce Steven and be with him instead when the kid was a bit older. People are so stupid."

The change in tone from when they'd first met Alana Templeton to what they were hearing was remarkable to Tim and Ashley both. In all previous interactions, Alana Templeton had presented as a well-spoken and normal person. That version of her appeared to have completely disintegrated as the questioning had developed.

"So you made contact with Mr. Medici to work on seducing him ... so that you could use him for the issue with getting the tiger out of the park?" Tim asked and saw Alana nod with almost a look of pride on her face. "And so that you could get him, in turn, to seduce Rayna Cunningham?" he asked and saw her nod again. "Why? Just so that he could hurt her?"

"Yeah, and I needed to be sure that she was the one before I did anything," Alana said.

"The one who ... Steven wanted to actually be with ... instead of you..."

"He told me, 'till death do us part'!" Alana exclaimed again. "He had no right to do that with that bitch - no right!"

As Ashley listened to the answers being provided, she wondered if they were actually getting anywhere. Alana Templeton had changed her demeanor enough to appear to be forthcoming in answering questions, but the answers she gave would make little sense to anyone sane.

"You really didn't care if the tiger attacked you - or worse?" Ashley asked.

"Me? No," Alana said. "But if he'd lost his son..."

"*Your* son too, Alana," Tim reminded her.

"He should feel the pain that I felt, knowing he's been screwing that woman," Alana said.

"*Was* screwing that woman," Tim corrected. "Do you think they're still seeing each other?"

"Wayne said they weren't," Alana replied. "I don't know if it's true or not."

"But why would Wayne lie to you?" asked Tim. "You said that he loves you."

At that moment, they saw Alana begin to shut down again. Neither agent was going to let that happen if they could help it.

"Tell us about the money, Alana," Ashley said. "We know that you completed courses that enabled you to grow your computer skills."

"Rayna did that," Alana began to say before seeming to take time to think of how to explain something. "She stole money. She should be put away for that."

"But … we know that, even though the account was taken out in her name, it wasn't Rayna who opened it, nor was it her who began the money skimming," said Tim. "You took courses to learn how to set up something that Rayna could be charged for."

"But your skills didn't quite extend far enough," Ashley surmised. "That was why you needed to find a hacker with more skills than you. So you found Liam Manson - a young guy just trying to set himself and his partner up for a better life with the child they have on the way."

"Threatened him and his unborn child, just so that you could set Rayna up to look guilty of something," Tim added. "How did you have Rayna's details to be able to open the account? How did you know who she was in the first place?"

"Found a bank card of hers in the pocket of a pair of Steven's pants," Alana said, her voice moving once more into a tone that sounded almost boastful. "That was the moment that I knew - I *knew* that he was screwing around. But I had something that he didn't know about - I had her name and her bank card. Used that to do what I had to do and then I put it back in his pocket and pretended I'd never seen it."

"Right, so please help me to understand, Alana," Tim said. "You did all of this, including drawing in all these extra people - Wayne, Liam, and Greg the vet too - so that you could make Rayna and Steven ... *pay* ... for having an affair?" he asked and saw her nod. "You didn't consider that by doing all of this, whether or not you survived that tiger attack, you would be giving them the ability to be open, and now be together as a happy couple, rid of you?"

Ashley and Tim both studied Alana's face as she considered that. It was clearly something she hadn't even thought about before. Both agents could see the moment of realization that the very thing that Alana had tried to stop from happening, she'd instead made entirely possible.

"I think we have enough for now," Ashley said as she and Tim stood and signaled for an officer to take her to a cell to wait for transport. "For the record," Ashley added before they left the room. "Any mother who puts their child in danger like you did, does not deserve to be a mother - ever."

# CHAPTER 31

"Well, Timmy Boy," Ashley said as the two of them sat in a restaurant near the hotel they'd been staying in. "I had no idea where this case was going to take us, but it did indeed turn out to be rather..."

"Interesting," both agents said, chuckling as they repeated the description that their boss, Sarah, had given them at the start.

"I still don't get how anyone could come up with that version of events in their head, to try and create some kind of scenario for revenge," Ashley said. "Makes absolutely no sense to me."

"I know," Tim agreed. "What gets me is that when she had made up that plan, she was able to manipulate other people to take part, and play so many roles to help her with her quest. Even going so far as to take out a new life insurance policy on herself, but fill out the form so that it looked like her husband *and* Rayna Cunningham had taken it out and would be beneficiaries of it. What kind of mind comes up with an idea like that?"

"Yeah, I guess she thought she'd worked out a solid plan, if only there hadn't been so many holes and areas of uncertainty in it," Ashley said as she pondered the absurdity of the entire situation.

"Agreed," said Tim. "But she was prepared for so many people to go down for the crime if she or Tony was hurt by this. Even the degree to which she got other people to do dirty work for her is amazing."

"Well, in their defense, Greg Samson and Liam Manson did act under threats made towards their families," said Ashley. "Having studied all the interactions recorded between everyone, we now know that they were both telling the truth about that."

"Yeah, but they're pretty lucky not to be charged with more than they are," said Tim.

"Revenge - I guess it can screw anybody up," Ashley said.

"Revenge and obsession," Tim said. "Steven Templeton ended his affair three years ago. During the past three years, there's no evidence to suggest he even heard from Rayna, let alone saw her. For that whole time, Alana had been waiting, obsessing, and planning to get revenge for it. All the efforts she went to in doing those courses over that entire time proved that. She wasn't just interested in learning about computers - she had that entire bizarre plan in her head all along. Crazy!"

"Maybe that's what love does to people," Ashley said, for a moment, wistful.

Tim studied her face. On occasion, she'd shared with him snippets of her inner desire to experience love, and to be a mother. Over and over, he found himself wanting to tell her that she could have both, if only she'd let herself. As always, he kept his thoughts on that subject to himself. They'd had a few moments when things had been hinted at. Those moments always only ended in discomfort. He appreciated her friendship, and he appreciated how easy it was for them to not only work together, but to do so very well. It was a recipe he never wanted to put out of balance by expressing how he felt about her.

"I suspect there's something more going on inside of Alana Templeton than simply loving her husband," said Tim. "The way that she manipulated everyone and did everything, including the training she said she got from Wayne about how to disable the tiger in the heat of the moment if she wanted to - unbelievable." He paused while he thought about the extent to which the woman had constructed the plan in her head, and how many scenarios she'd considered as a way to get revenge on her husband. "Can someone even claim to love their partner if they're prepared to put children in so much risk?"

"I think that's what has gotten to me most of all about this case, Tim," Ashley said, looking closely at him. "How can anyone risk their child's life like that? She talked as though she *wanted* Tony to be attacked and killed."

"Yeah, she did sound remarkably weird when it came to the kids," Tim agreed. "Like they were some necessary evil that Steven wanted but she never did."

"But she looked so loving when we saw her at the house…"

"As we both well know and often say, some people are just really good actors," Tim said, shrugging. "You and I know that more than many people. We see actors almost every day in our job. These people, who can commit the worst crimes but then smile and be charming - that, to me, is an entirely different kind of human being to what you and I are, Ash. They're even more dangerous because of their ability to act like chameleons and blend in with people who could very well become their next prey."

"Hmm," Ashley said as she finished off her final cup of coffee. "Alright, well, shall we hit the road? I'm eager to get home…"

"And shut yourself away from the world," Tim said, finishing her sentence. "Yeah, I know, Special Agent Ashley Power. You need to get into your quiet place of solitude."

Ashley grinned at him as they stood. While she was aware that he felt a bit more towards her than partners usually did on the job, she was still glad that he was who she got to work with most of the time. They had a good working relationship. On the rare occasion when she tried to view him as an outsider would, she sometimes imagined that he might be a good choice…

"Let's do it," she heard Tim say. "I'll drive, shall I?" he asked to tease her and try and break her out of her quiet contemplation.

"As if," was all that Ashley had to say to make them both laugh. Another case was over with. After she got home and took her usual time out, she would be primed and ready to embark upon another one. It was always the way. It was how she lived her life - and she loved it.

*The End*

OTHER BOOKS
BY
ANN M PRATLEY

A POWER MOORE INVESTIGATION TALE
HOONIGAN
ANN M PRATLEY

# HOONIGAN

Tristan Clarkson has woken up, over and over, bound to a chair and unable to see. He has no idea where he is, or why he is in the situation he's woken to. His memory is vague, protecting him from recent events that will eventually haunt him for the rest of his life. He wants to remember, but at the same time his mind acts as though he really, really doesn't. Initially he's confused. With each waking, his memory clears that little bit more, as do his senses. He soon becomes aware that the very person who has abducted him is in the room with him, determined to make Tristan pay for something he cannot even remember.

Meanwhile, in a hospital nearby a patient has been taken. With the help of Special Agents Ashley Power and Tim Moore, an investigation begins into where the man has been taken, and who would have reason to remove him. With the patient having already been weak from time in a coma, time is of the essence in finding him alive.

Hoonigan is a blend of crime and suspense, intermingled with the strength of friendship, and the awakening of one father's realization of just how much his son really means to him.

A POWER MOORE INVESTIGATION TALE
RESOLUTION
of
HAPPINESS
ANN M PRATLEY

# RESOLUTION OF HAPPINESS

Fiona Thompson - better known as Flo to everyone who knew her - took a plunge and stepped out of her comfort zone and into the world of online dating. With persistence she found her prince. He ticked all the boxes. He was handsome. He was financially secure. He loved her. He married her.

She was warned by friends and family that there was something off about him. She didn't listen.

Then she woke up cold, inside the darkness of a wooden box.

Join Special Agents Ashley Power and Tim Moore as they investigate the disappearance of Flo, going on a surprising journey that nobody in Flo's world could possibly anticipate

A POWER MOORE INVESTIGATION TALE
HOME BY THE SEA
ANN M PRATLEY

# HOME BY THE SEA

A decade ago, homeless people began disappearing from four neighboring towns. Day to day, the commuters making their way to and from work never took notice of the less fortunate they passed. They didn't notice as the number of homeless reduced. They didn't even notice when entire groups of homeless people vanished.

A young woman, eager to find out where her grandfather disappeared to, began trying to find him. When four police departments dismissed her, telling her that her grandfather would no doubt turn up when he wanted to, she was too young to realize she should pursue the matter further.

Now, ten years on, she's stepped up and pushed harder for something to be done to find not only her grandfather but also the countless other people who seemed to have disappeared around the same time.

Called in to investigate the disappearances, Special Agents Ashley Power and Tim Moore find themselves searching for - and finding - so much more than they thought they would

ANN M PRATLEY
Alessandra
Chisholm Manor
Book 1

# ALESSANDRA

After receiving news from her parents of a possible betrothal, Alessandra, an 18 year old with an ingrained belief that no-one would ever wish to marry her, finds herself in a love so great that at times she cannot breathe.

Married to someone as inexperienced as herself, she finds herself on a sexual journey of learning and exploration.

The combination of their mutual inexperience contributes to Alessandra discovering a degree of emotional and physical love that she has never before realized could exist.

That love will be tested by someone from her past with sinister intentions. Jealous of the physical love Alessandra shares with her husband, he is set on doing whatever it takes to have the woman he desires, no matter the cost.

ANN M PRATLEY
Finding
Himself
Again

# FINDING HIMSELF AGAIN

In a small seaside area of Australia, 28-year-old Tom Santini has recently returned to the outside world after ten years in jail following an error of judgment in his youth. Readjustment hasn't been easy but luck has taken a turn for him. The woman that his brother, Graham, has been seeing is a woman with connections. Through her, Tom has finally found an employer who will give an ex-criminal a chance to start over. It hasn't been easy since his release, but Tom is learning to face his situation with reality and step up to take responsibility for his decisions.

Settled in his job at Toby's Stop'n'Dine, Tom's attention is captured by a young woman who enters. She's beautiful and alluring but, seeing and talking to her, he can deeply sense her being on the run from something … or someone.

Cat is smart, sexy and a woman who will make him wonder if he does have a chance at being happy in love, despite his past. But why does she spook so easily? Tom knows that whatever happens, he has to think before he acts. He's determined to do things differently when dealing with difficult situations. He's already missed out on so much.

What can he do to calm and keep safe the woman who he so recently  met but already has made a difference in his life? How can he save the woman with a deep-seated passion that drives him crazy…

The woman who understands just how important and difficult it is to find oneself again …

# ANN M PRATLEY

# Knight of Desire

# KNIGHT OF DESIRE

Cecily, Rohesia and Maynard have grown up together from childhood. In many ways they've always felt equal ... except for Maynard being a prince, that is.

After her two closest friends find each other in love and then marriage, taking on the ruling of a kingdom, Cecily finds herself questioning if love is in her future. Over time, it becomes apparent that she certainly has caught someone's eye. He is a knight and he is known to be a rogue, but can the handsome Sir Henry capture the fair heart of Cecily, and push her fears aside?

*~~Knight of Desire is a simple old-fashioned short-read romance. There is no adult content or violence in this story.*

# ANN M PRATLEY

# Blade of Envy

A FOUR SWORDS NOVEL - BOOK 1

BLADE OF ENVY
(FOUR SWORDS SERIES - BOOK #1)

***They expected quite a different kind of destruction...***

In the realm of the House of Mordasini, the three royal offspring of King Maynard and Queen Azura are beginning their journeys into adulthood.

As the eldest, Prince Aldin, starts to obsess about his future role as the next king, so also begins an obsession about his younger brother. Torn between wanting to be the one who rules over everyone else, but also wanting the life that is being set up for his brother, Aldin begins a journey of envy that grows darker as time passes.

Meanwhile, as one brother ruminates about the life of the other, their younger sister, Princess Semera, appears to grow ill. In the quiet of her deep slumber, something surprising begins to happen as, from a distance, she unknowingly becomes someone else's focus.

# ANN M PRATLEY

# Blade of Love

## A FOUR SWORDS NOVEL - BOOK 2

BLADE OF LOVE
(FOUR SWORDS SERIES - BOOK #2)

In the kingdom of the House of Mordasini, a future king is waiting for the day to come when his father will die. While there's nothing to suggest that King Maynard will be leaving this world anytime soon, his oldest son, Aldin, increasingly desires to be the one on the throne.

With the darkness that has been residing in his soul since he was a child, ideas begin to flow inside of Aldin's mind. All around him, there are things happening that go against his idea of how the realm should be run. In particular, the realization that his father has granted permission to his brother, Prince Iztal, to wed is something that adds to Aldin's hatred for his brother - a hatred that has grown into an intense obsession.

While brothers continue to share their volatile relationship, their sister continues to experience signs that a beast will soon arrive in the realm, eager to cause destruction. Everyone thinks they are ready for the beast's return, but are they?

# FREEDOM OF FLIGHT

# CHRISTIAN

ANN M PRATLEY

1

CHRISTIAN
(FREEDOM OF FLIGHT SERIES - BOOK #1)

Twenty four year old Christian Shaw has a good life.
He's had a rocky ride with being charged for a crime
he didn't commit, but he's come out on the other side,
older and wiser. He has good friends who've stood by
him. He has family who love him. However there's
something about Christian that he's never understood.
There's something about him that sets him apart. It
has made him not want to get close to anyone.

Now someone's appeared unexpectedly. To his
surprise, she's just like him. Even more importantly,
she has the knowledge to help him understand more
about the strange existence he lives. But is she as nice
as she appears, or could she have a darker reason for
seeking him out and devoting time to him?

Providing an insight into one man's strange journey of
coming to grips with who he really is, 'Christian' tells
a story of courage, friendship and
crime solving intrigue.

FREEDOM
OF
FLIGHT
BRANDON
ANN M PRATLEY
2

## BRANDON
## (FREEDOM OF FLIGHT SERIES - BOOK #2)

For fifteen years, Brandon McStevens has held himself away from everyone he knew prior to the day he turned fourteen. That day changed his life forever. Something happened to him that he can't explain to anyone. He feels ashamed and embarrassed. The only way he's ever been able to move past that and live, has been to find somewhere else to reside.

Since leaving his family home, he has continued to live in a small cave. Nestled high above a small coastal community, he has come to spend most of his time enjoying the ocean … oh, and up in the sky. He doesn't know how it happened. He doesn't know *why* it happened. All he knows is that despite understanding how much hurt he must have caused when he left home all those years ago, he now lives the only existence he can imagine.

He's never met anyone like him. He's never *seen* anyone like him. Until that day when that woman and her dog saw him change, no-one had ever seen or heard of him doing that. To this day he regrets having shown himself like he did. But time passed and it has all been forgotten … or has it?

Certain he's the only one like himself, he's surprised when two people come looking for him … and have much to tell him. Finally the time will come when he no longer has to feel like a freak of nature … or so alone.

FREEDOM
OF
FLIGHT
TRINITY
ANN M PRATLEY
3

TRINITY
(FREEDOM OF FLIGHT SERIES - BOOK #3)

A strange series of events have been happening in cities around the southwest of the country. When one bank is robbed on a small scale, it makes the banking professionals and law enforcement curious. When a second, then a third, then a fourth are also robbed without anyone knowing how it's been done, agencies combine resources to begin the search to find out who has been doing it and how.

Trinity Love is a twenty-five-year-old woman who's been surviving week to week, doing what she can to find money for her next meal and a roof over her head. In a unique way, she needs neither. She has a level of survival instinct built into her that should enable her to live a good life on the straight and narrow. That kind of life is one that she's never wanted or sought.

Seeing the latest news broadcast about the bank thefts, Brandon McStevens notices something about it that catches his attention. Talking to his new friends, Kelly and Christian, they decide it might be worth investigating.

Embarking on their new journey of exploration to find others like them, Christian and Kelly are faced with a new type of person they've never met before. Trinity is challenging in so many ways, but is she open to meeting people like her?

# FORBIDDEN CONFLICTS
## SERIES

Forbidden Conflicts
Book 1
Amethyst
of Youth
ANN M PRATLEY

AMETHYST OF YOUTH
(FORBIDDEN CONFLICTS SERIES - BOOK #1)

The youngest member of the Stonewarden family, Charlotte (Charlie), is 18 years old. As with everyone in her family when they reach that age, she's been told that when she turns 19, she'll be recruited into the family business. She has her warning that she has one year to do anything else she wishes to do - travel, study, work. Whatever she wants to do, she has 365 days to do it. On her next birthday, her life will stop being her own.

But Charlie wants nothing to do with the business. The youngest of six, with five older brothers, she wants a different life. Maybe if the family business was something normal like a retail shop or a business centered around trade, she'd feel differently. There are people who say that her family's long term history of robbing from the rich and providing to the poor is a good thing. To her, all she can see is that they are thieves. Plain and simple.

Her view is further secured when she and her older brother, Max, are shot at in a local supermarket. Seeing Max lying in blood and later lying unmoving in hospital in a coma, pushes her further in her resolve to find a way to not take part in the activities of her father and brothers.

At the shootout she is saved by a checkout operator, Ash. Whilst building their friendship Charlie will learn things about her family that she didn't particularly wish to know. She will hear more and more that she can't share with Ash, and the more she learns, the wider the gap will become.

In years she's young, but having lost her mother when she was only nine years old, Charlie has an older soul. The possibilities she'll be presented with during her one final year of her own, will push her in her considerations of how she really wants her life to be. She wants one thing. Her strict ex-military father wants another. The dynamics of her new friendship will pull her in a third direction.

How will she chose what's right for her? What would she have to do to break free from the chains that her father wants to place around her?

## REVIEWERS SAY:

*"This was a good clean romance with plenty of action to further the story along ... will make you ponder about life's situations, their actions and reactions, and how the decisions of past generations can affect the current ones. You'll be glad you read it!"*

*"... loved this book! It took me by surprise--great from start to finish! I don't normally read crime family dramas, but I love NA/coming-of-age novels. Charlie is on the cusp of being inducted into her family's Robin Hood-esque biz, but she doesn't want that. She isn't sure what, exactly, she does want...just not THAT. Her connection with Ash furthers that disconnect, and they stumble through the beginnings of young love together. Of course, secrets and family craziness threaten their romance at every turn. ...It's an awesome start to the Forbidden Conflicts series!"*

*"A wonderful read. A timeless push and pull between our own wants and our family's wants. Will she follow the path her family wants or will she follow her own path? Read the book to find out."*

Forbidden Conflicts
Book 2
Ruby
of Law
ANN M PRATLEY

RUBY OF LAW
(FORBIDDEN CONFLICTS SERIES - BOOK #2)

For generations the Leadbetters have lived off crime.
For as long as any of them know, fathers and mothers
have taught sons and daughters how to succeed in the
criminal world, primarily through theft.

Phillip Leadbetter is 29 and has devoted his whole
life so far to doing what his father and mother have
told him to do. The sacrifice for doing that is that he
still lives at home and he hasn't yet met anyone who
he believes could accept the man that he is, because
of his family.

One night a potential tragedy brings him into the path
of Daisy, an up and coming professional in the legal
sector. Seeing him as her knight in shining armor, she
can't stop thinking about the rugged guy who saved
her. She's also very pleased when fate brings their
paths to cross again.

Getting to know one another, both leave out major
details about who they are. She doesn't want him to
know she's a lawyer because some people just don't
like lawyers. He doesn't want to tell her about his
family and their long history of criminal activity.

How then will things turn when they meet up in a
courthouse, each learning in that moment who the
other really is? How will they deal with the fact that
she is on one side of the law, and he is very
definitely on the other?

Forbidden Conflicts
Book 3
Diamond
of War
ANN M PRATLEY

DIAMOND OF WAR
(FORBIDDEN CONFLICTS SERIES - BOOK #3)

James Stonewarden is a playboy. He has been since the moment he first started to notice girls. He loves them all, and they all love him. Why would he want to get himself into a relationship?

Sasha Leadbetter's a hot-headed young woman, known to the law for her quick temper and harsh ways. She isn't one to mess with - especially with the way she keeps a blade in her pocket. To her it's her security. It's something that makes her feel safe and comfortable. She's had it for so long that it's nothing for her to pull it out and hold it to someone's throat without any conscious thought.

Unaware of who each other are, or how their families are distantly interconnected through crime, the chance of James Stonewarden meeting Sasha Leadbetter is slim. But it happens.

A playboy and a young woman who has the mentality to kill. What kind of recipe could that result in? And what will happen when James identifies a car at Sasha's family home, that matches the description his sister Charlie gave after the supermarket shooting months earlier?

Forbidden Conflicts
Book 4
Sapphire
of Prejudice
ANN M PRATLEY

SAPPHIRE OF PREJUDICE
(FORBIDDEN CONFLICTS SERIES - BOOK #4)

Greg and Rhett. They've grown up together since they were teenagers. They've fought together. They've stolen together. They've even loved women together. But something deeper has existed in one of them for years. He's hidden it well. Being part of the great Leadbetter gang and family, the prejudice of certain situations has always been loudly expressed by many of its members - too many, and certainly enough to make anyone fearful of what would happen if feelings were revealed and brought out into the open.

A night has passed when finally, in a moment of wondering if he'd survive till morning, Rhett's taken the chance and kissed the person of his desire. Given their circumstances, what can they do, and where can they go?

Meanwhile, as Phillip Leadbetter continues on his path of happiness with his Daisy, someone from her past has grown obsessed with her and wants her back. To what degree will he put into effect a plan to get her back, and get Phillip out of her life forever?

*~~ NOTE: This book does contain adult sexual content and LOTS of swear words.*

Forbidden Conflicts
Book 5
Emerald
of Wisdom
ATLEY

EMERALD OF WISDOM
(FORBIDDEN CONFLICTS SERIES - BOOK #5)

When Mitchell Stonewarden lost his wife to cancer more than a decade ago, he vowed to never give his heart to anyone else. With all of his children now adults, and a new generation of Stonewardens having already begun, he's finally started to wonder - does he really want to be alone for the rest of his life? The handover of the family business to his oldest son, Vic, has seemed to be free of difficulty or issues - but has it? Mitchell knows little of his oldest son's private life away from the family. He is surprised by what is brought to his attention that he had no idea about.

While Mitchell finally starts to move on into a new chapter of his life, another of his sons - Max - is on his own path of discovery in life and in love. Previously well-known as 'Romeo' to his family and peers, he begins to wonder if Christy - a surprising addition to his life - has grown to become more important to him than any other young woman he's ever met. When her work at a homeless shelter tests the boundaries of her safety, Max's commitment to her is also tested, making him wonder if he will, indeed, end up hurting her.

Meanwhile, on the other side of town, the Leadbetter family is shattered by an unexpected turn of events that leaves Stacey wondering if she is going to lose the man she's loved for more than three decades...

# PAINFUL
## DELIVERANCE
### ANN M PRATLEY

## PAINFUL DELIVERANCE
## (PAINFUL DELIVERANCE SERIES - BOOK #1)

*She just wasn't made to inflict pain.*

She knows it is nothing abnormal. She knows others enjoy it. But with every new level of pain he directs her to deliver to him, Alexis feels another piece of her soul die. He has wealth and he has power, and she knows he won't easily let her go.

But she has to leave. Escape. Move on. Forget. She has reached her limit of what she can do. The plans are in place to get away. She just has to hope that wherever she goes - whoever she meets - she won't find herself in exactly the same situation again.

# DARKNESS OF HEART

## ANN M PRATLEY

# DARKNESS OF HEART
## (PAINFUL DELIVERANCE SERIES - BOOK #2)

*She thought he'd stopped looking. He hadn't.*

She got away from him to start a new life. She moved on. But in his mind, he still loves her and needs her. He still believes that she loves him. That she is meant to be his. That he is meant to be hers.

He will not give up searching for her. He will not give up *fighting* for her. He will pursue her and stop at nothing to get her back. But it will come at a cost … a sacrifice much greater than he will see coming. A sacrifice that will finally wake him up and bring him back to stark reality.

REVIEWERS SAY:

*"... author did a great job of making brief references from the first book. Lincoln, Lexi and Alexis are back, though perhaps the most complex character is Diana ... definitely written for a mature audience ... the author is a great storyteller and writes with an easy to read style ... certainly writes a more interesting and readable story than many best-selling authors. It's very easy for me to recommend this book with 5 of 5 stars."*

*"This story continued the journey of Alexis, Anthony and Lincoln while giving us a new perspective into the repercussions of Lincoln and Alexis's relationship: from the POV of Lincoln's wife Diana! I loved her addition to the story's ... kept the tension of the story just right, balancing the calm new life Alexis has been building and keeping the reader engaged."*

*"It is a book of courage, the courage to leave everything you know behind, the courage to change, the courage to face your fears, and the courage to face the unknown."*

# FRIENDSHIP OF DESIRE

## ANN M PRATLEY

# FRIENDSHIP OF DESIRE
## (PAINFUL DELIVERANCE SERIES - BOOK #3)

Tom and Samantha. Feisty friends from childhood who feel like they know each other inside out, until the day comes when one of them suggests they go to a BDSM club together, and become formal play partners. Pushing the limits of what each of them can individually stand in their lifelong friendship, they attract and repel like magnets, until the time comes when they must choose how they will relate to one another - and what kind of relationship they will go on to have in the future.

Whilst on this journey of discovery, the two of them meet and make a new friend - Alexis. A young woman with a hidden and secretive past, and a mystery surrounding the relationship she has - or has had - with a renowned business entrepreneur who begins to integrate himself into Samantha's life, unknown to any of them whether he has done it for him, or for her … or for Alexis, being the mysterious link from his past.

REVIEWERS SAY:
*"While this book is billed as the third in a series, I would classify it more as a spin-off ... I enjoyed this book. Samantha and Tom's relationship was sweet. Their exploration and experimentation, and how it stressed the boundaries of their (frustratingly) platonic friendship was fun to read about. Fans of Ms. Pratley's first books in the Painful Deliverance series will surely enjoy this more intimate peek into Samantha and Tom's relationship."*

1
THE
Golden
DESIRES
ANN M PRATLEY

THE GOLDEN DESIRES
(THE GOLDEN DESIRES SERIES - BOOK #1)

When Isabella starts to dream of a stranger, she's awakened inside with feelings she has never felt before. She knows he's not someone she's ever seen before, and he is not of her village. He is a stranger, and she's desperate to determine if he is real or he is a part of her imagination.

Far away, a businessman desperate to escape the city noise and stress embarks on a journey to find peace and the solitude he increasingly needs and desires. But at his destination he will find much, much more.

REVIEWERS SAY:

*"I found myself drawn to keep reading ... almost as if reading a compelling action/adventure because the pacing was so excellent. And... ahem... the love scenes are quite well written, too ... I look forward to reading the sequel..."*

*"The author paints such a vivid picture of life in this idyllic community that one begins to think it may actually exist ... extremely well-written ... perfect for anyone who is looking for a romance with a hint of paranormal mystery."*

*"The concept behind this story was intriguing and very sexy ... Fireworks and all out romance, followed by some interesting obstacles, but they are overcome, because well...it's love. What I loved about this read was the fairytale like narration with a sci-fi/fantasy kick; it made me feel like I was part of the story..."*

*"... magical quality was a nice twist, delving into the realm of fantasy romance ... the author's style was well suited to the tone of the world she has created. Did it leave me hungry for the next installment? Absolutely!"*

# THE Golden SUPREMACY

## ANN M PRATLEY

THE GOLDEN SUPREMACY
(THE GOLDEN DESIRES SERIES - BOOK #2)

*What is lying in wait, eager to destroy them?*

Over distance and time they met and fell in love, choosing to live together in an ancient village of peace and harmony. And then the battle had happened. A fight between good and evil; the warmth of fire and the cold of ice. They thought they had won. But had they?

Trent and Isabella start to feel that the entity that had tried to destroy them, might not have been defeated after all. But rather, perhaps it is lying in wait for another opportunity to strike.

What is it?
And who is its puppet now?

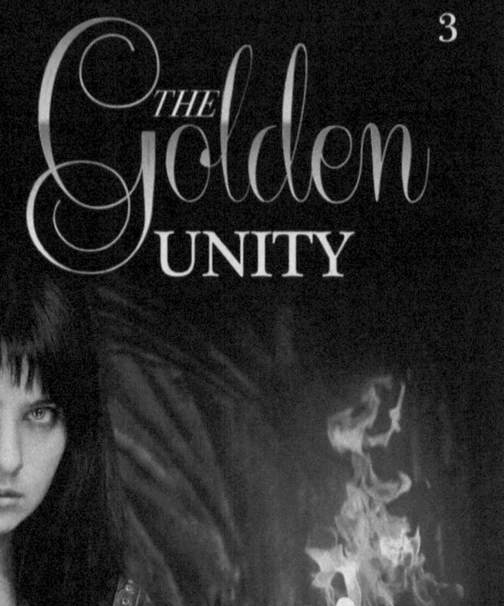
3
THE
Golden
UNITY
ANN M PRATLEY

THE GOLDEN UNITY
(GOLDEN DESIRES SERIES - BOOK #3)

Cesare is the golden child of the village. His brilliant yellow hair is unlike the color of anyone else's. He is a cheerful child who, in the eyes of some, can do no wrong.

Esmeralda is the product of two biological parents who have something buried deep within them. Something that makes them easy to manipulate by the being that has not given up on wanting to destroy the ancient village. The young lass with the blue-black hair is looked upon as an alternative child. She captures attention and intrigues the villagers. When they look at her, sometimes they feel like they're looking at a puzzle that confuses them and they cannot solve. It's impossible to determine why but there's just something *different* about Esmeralda.

Despite them being opposites in nature and appearance, the two have grown up together as best friends, just as their parents did before them. The goodness of Cesare showers a level of kindness and friendship on Esmeralda that she has never been able to turn away from. The difference of Esmeralda has always held Cesare's attention. Between them they have found a balance that holds them together as friends.

But what will happen as they move into their time as young adults? They are unknowing as yet that they are meant to be paired, whilst at the same time they are meant to be adversaries.

What does the puppet master have planned now? And

how will these two gifted youth react to someone trying to manipulate them against their will?

A third strike from the puppet master. Will it win in its plan of attack this time?

TOTAL FREEDOM
SERIES

# ANN M PRATLEY

# *Total* FREEDOM

## TOTAL FREEDOM
## (TOTAL FREEDOM SERIES - BOOK #1)

For Debbie King, life began feeling like it was all too difficult, she would never achieve, she would never have friends, and she would simply never fit in. But when she meets someone new who seems just like her, with low self-esteem and no belief in themselves and what they have to offer, Debbie finds strength to focus more on them and less on herself.

So begins an incredible journey of friendship and love that will be tested by other people entering their world, and the shared passion they have for their musical talents and career together. It is a deep friendship that will be tested over and over again by events and an ongoing uncertainty over what their relationship really should really be like.

REVIEWERS SAY:

*"The overall story was great and hooked me right in. I had to stay with them for the entire journey ... you know it's a good story when you wish it didn't have to end."*

*"... an incredible job developing complex characters that are emotionally scarred and then allowing the reader to really understand their pain ... a terrific coming of age story surrounding a triangle of young characters, Debbie, Craig and Steven."*

*"Covered a lot of different things that can happen as we grow and was appealing for that reason."*

# ANN M PRATLEY

# Total New
# BEGINNINGS

TOTAL NEW BEGINNINGS
(TOTAL FREEDOM SERIES - BOOK #2)

In her early adulthood Debbie made a choice. She had two men who loved her. She chose one. She lost the friendship of the other.

Twenty years on, horrific tragedy strikes. Mother to three grown children, she has to find the strength to be there for them, while pushing her own grief aside. Dealing with the loss of the man who has been by her side for two decades pushes her into depression. Every day seems harder to deal with than the last. The feeling of loss is further heightened by finding her husband's lifetime of journals. Hesitant at first to look inside them, she eventually does. Almost instantly she regrets that decision. In the years of her husband's writing she reads things that lead her to seriously question whether she ever really knew him at all, or if they had actually been strangers for two decades.

The combination of the loss of her husband, and the uncertainty about who he really was, pushes her to retire into a dark room and have no desire to leave. She wants to shut out the world. She wants to not believe what she knows in her heart is reality.

With her youngest daughter, Poppy, still living at home, Debbie is eventually pulled from the darkness by her daughter's pleas. Finally the dark days start to fade and Debbie can start to see the sun shining once more. Finally she can find the strength to keep going. Finally she can start to move into a period of recovery and growth. Finally she can accept that it's okay to accept help and lean on others.

As she starts rediscovering her ability to embrace life again, results appear from her daughter's determination to help her mother. Someone from her past is brought back into her life. A friendship is re-established. It's time to let go of the past and begin a new future. It's time for total new beginnings.

Did you ever hear the words in your head … 'what if'? What if you chose one path earlier in life but later had the chance to walk down the path previously unchosen? Would you?

www.ingramcontent.com/pod-product-compliance
Lightning Source LLC
Chambersburg PA
CBHW030926210726

48290CB00007B/2092